My name is Loa

A Story of Exile, Adventure, and Romance on The Island of Moloka'i

Written by
Dorothea N. Buckingham

ISLAND HERITAGE

My Name Is Loa
A Story of Exile, Adventure, and Romance on The Island of Moloka'i

Written by Dorothea N. Buckingham
Edited by Virginia Wageman
Illustrated by Snowden Hodges
Designed by Wayne Shek

Published by

 ISLAND HERITAGE
P U B L I S H I N G

99-880 Iwaena Street
Aiea, Hawaii 96701
(808) 487-7299
E-mail: hawaii4u@islandheritage.com

ISBN NO. 0-89610-337-4
First Edition, First Printing – 1999

For Evelyn

Contents

Illustrations: *Page 6, 17, 34, 42, 54, 67, 71, and 100.*

 *Introduction*

In the mid-1800s Hansen's disease, an illness once known as leprosy, became epidemic in Hawai`i. Some people said the Chinese brought the sickness to the islands, a few missionaries said it was a plague from God, and there were several doctors who claimed it was the fourth stage of syphilis.

Leprosy is a disfiguring disease, and in those days it was always fatal. In Europe during that time, Hansen's disease patients were isolated from the public—put in special hospitals. But in Hawai`i the idea of separating the sick from their families was against the most basic of Hawaiian values.

Leprosy touched everyone. By the late 1800s one of every thirty-nine Hawaiians was effected by the disease. A Lahaina relative of Queen Emma was one of the first to be diagnosed, later so was her father. And Peter Ka`eo, her cousin, was even sent to Moloka`i for a time.

No one knew what caused leprosy or how it was spread. The fear of contagion spread and suspicions grew. As more people died, the movement to isolate the sick gained popularity. Ministers quoted the Bible to support banishing them. Honolulu politicians warned about the cost of treating them. Frightened families with sick members began leaving the cities and hiding in the mountains. But still, there was a resistance to round up those who were ill.

Then, in 1865, only months after he ascended the throne, King Kamehameha V (Lot) approved an Act to Prevent the Spread of Leprosy. By this act persons with Hansen's disease were isolated.

Originally, land in the Pâlolo Valley on O`ahu was set aside as a confinement settlement. But when Makiki residents protested about the possible contamination of their water supply, an off-O`ahu site was named. The land finally chosen for the settlement was a remote peninsula on Moloka`i.

Over the course of the next thirty years, tens of thousands of people were diagnosed with the disease. Most were sent to Moloka`i. The chosen site was on a flat piece of land formed at the base of the Moloka`i cliffs. It is a forbidding place. It protrudes into the ocean, unprotected from wind and rain and encircled by cliffs that block out the sun.

Conditions at the settlement changed with the arrival of Father Damien DeVeuster in May 1873. Damien tried to establish moral order. He taught Christian values, tended to the sick, built them homes, repaired existing buildings, made coffins, dug graves, and prayed the prayers for the dead. He also drew the attention of the Hawaiian royalty to the needs of the patients. In 1881 Lili`uokalani, then a Princess of Hawai`i, visited Kalaupapa and met Father Damien. In 1884 she returned as Queen.

When Damien died in April 1889 there were others who continued his work including the Sacred Hearts brothers and priests, Mother Marianne Kopp, and the Sisters of the Third Order of Saint Francis. Among those who remained was a layman named Ira Dutton. Damien called him Brother Joseph.

Before he died Damien saw the building of the Bishop Home for Girls and the Baldwin Home for Boys, dormitories that were established because so many of the patients were children. Bishop Home, at Kalaupapa, was under the care of Mother Marianne. Baldwin Home, on the opposite side of the peninsula, was under Joseph Dutton's care. By the early 1900s there were baseball leagues, boxing clubs, and acrobatic teams and a band.

My Name Is Loa is about a fifteen-year-old boy who was sent to Baldwin Home. It is not a true story. There is no record of a William Maka`ike Alaloa Ka`ai at Kalawao, but the description of his life at the settlement is true. The menu in the dining hall, the runaway bull, the escapes, the weddings, the funerals are all a matter of record.

In 1898, the year this story takes place, the Hawaiian islands were annexed to the United States, and in 1900, when Hawai`i was organized as a Territory of the United States, all persons who were citizens of the Republic of Hawai`i became citizens of both Hawai`i and the United States. The Annexation Commission's visit to Moloka`i described in this book is based on fact.

There are a few historical inaccuracies—the storm described in the book took place years earlier, and the stories about Brother Dutton are all fiction.

But for the most part you can believe what you read, if you remember, this is not a history book, this is Loa's story.

Chapter 1

The Disease That Tears Families Apart

Ma`i oka`a wale `ohana

It looked a festive occasion. Horse-drawn carriages lined the dock and lei sellers sat on the sidewalk selling their wares. The Royal Band played, a church choir sang. There was even a representative from the Queen. Girls in long dresses with ribbons in their hair and boys in knickers ran through the crowd, while men in black suits and women in fine hats strolled hand-in-hand.

I had on my new gray suit. My brother, Keo, was in knickers. I remember the cuffs of my jacket scratching the back of my hand. I remember the coarseness of the wool and the smoothness of the satin lining.

It was late in the afternoon on Sunday, March 6, my shipment day. The smell of roasting pig and the stench of the harbor mixed with the sweet perfume of the flower lei. There were about twenty of us being shipped to Moloka`i that day. Most of us were men, a few were old women. There were two little girls, holding hands, clutching on to their cotton dolls.

I wasn't afraid, I was numb. I wasn't sure what was going to happen. I tried not to watch as the sun inched its way to the horizon. At sunset we would sail.

The *Mokoli`i's* captain ordered the gangplank to be lowered. It was getting harder not to be scared. The ship's wench screeched and the gangplank banged against the dock. The sheriff stood on an overturned crate and cleared his throat as he opened a manila folder marked "Patient Photos." He took out the photos and handed them to his waiting deputies. The deputies roamed through the crowd, matching the Board of Health photos with our faces.

The sun had almost set.

The ship's crew prodded the cattle up the gangplank. I kept my gaze on the cows, avoiding the deputy coming toward me. As he moved closer, I felt my father's hands on my shoulders. The deputy pressed a photo next to my cheek, then he moved on without a word.

The *Mokoli`i's* captain signaled the sheriff to begin boarding the patients. The sheriff put on his glasses and read the first name. "Ikaika Keale."

A woman screamed. The sheriff looked up. Two deputies were already moving toward Keale. The woman clung to Keale, pressing her body against his. A deputy grabbed her arm to pull her away.

"Leave her alone," Keale yelled.

The woman jabbed her elbow into the deputy and twisted away, but she wasn't strong enough to overpower him.

A boy, no more than eight, jumped up on the deputy's back, pounding him with punches. The first deputy raised his club and swung it at the boy.

"No!" Keale screamed. "Not my son!" There was a crack of the club. The boy fell to the dock, and the woman tore loose from the deputy and kneeled to cradle the boy in her arms.

"'Aulani," Keale called the woman's name. "'Aulani, *aloha nō*," he said. I love you.

The roll call continued. One after another women in long dresses and men in black suits climbed the gangplank of the Mokoli`i. The hull of the ship smashed against the dock. The march continued. Some of the patients boarded the ship looking straight ahead. They never turned back. Others were prodded like cattle.

What was at first just one or two voices crying out in grief was now a chorus. The great kanikau, the wailing of my people, filled the night. It drowned out the hymns of the choir and called on the gods for mercy.

Then I heard it, "William Maka`ike Alaloa Ka`ai."

My name.

"William Maka`ike Alaloa Ka`ai."

It was like a blow to my chest. I couldn't breathe. I couldn't hear. Everything stopped. A deputy headed toward me.

This can't be, I thought. This can't be.

My father took me into his arms and held me tight. His chest was heaving and I could hear him breathing. "Where is the justice, Jehovah?" he screamed. "Where is the justice?"

I saw the deputy's eyes—they were dead, gray eyes. I closed my eyes and let myself sink into my father's arms. I wanted Papa to hold me. I wanted him to save me, to hide me in the mountains, to fight off the deputies, to make life go back to what it was and make me clean again, like before the *lēpela*.

"Help me, Papa," I whispered.

You're my father, I thought. You are supposed to make things right.

He pressed my head to his chest, and I felt his tears on my hair.

Why didn't you hide me, Papa? I thought. Why didn't you take me to the mountains? You could have smuggled me to Kaua`i.

"Why didn't you take me to the mountains?" I whispered no louder than my breath.

"Help us, Jehovah!" Papa cried.

You didn't fight for me. You just gave me up.

Papa stroked my hair and kissed my forehead. He held my face in his hands. He opened his mouth to speak but no sound came out, only his gasping for air.

It was then that Mama stepped forward. She stood tall in front of me. Her hair was piled on her head in a bun and she was wearing a high-necked dress as black as her eyes. At her neck she wore an Italian cameo given to her by the Queen.

"Forgive me, son," she whispered.

"There's nothing to forgive," I said. But there was, and we both knew it. It was because of her blood that I got the *lēpela*. It was she who carried the Ka`eo blood—a royal blood line with a history of the disease.

I bowed my head as she placed a *maile* lei on my shoulder. She drew me close and I rested my head on her bosom. As I closed my eyes I remembered when I was a child, when she took me for picnics. Sometimes I would get too tired to walk, or get frightened by a mongoose, and she would pick me up in her arms and I would curl my legs around her waist and she would hold me tight and carry me back to the buggy.

I wanted her to carry me away now. I wanted her to beg the Queen for a favor.

Why didn't she? I thought.

I put my ear to my mother's chest and listened for the sound of her heart. I breathed in the musk of the *maile*, fresh from the mountains.

I'm afraid, Mama. Do you know that I'm afraid?

Her arms surrounded me.

"*Pua `ole ke aloha,*" she said. Love never fails.

But it had failed—I was sailing for Kalaupapa. Mama let go of me, almost pushing me away. Tears rolled down her cheek, getting caught in the lines in her face. I wanted her to save me—but I knew I couldn't be saved.

I leaned down and kissed my brother Keo. Keo's body was thin, like mine, but his body was clean.

Why me? I thought. Of all of us in the family, why did this happen to me?

Keo looked up at me and smiled.

Who will protect you, Keo, if you get the *lēpela*? What will they do for you?

"I love you, brother," I said.

"I love you." He smiled.

Two Board of Health deputies flanked me and gripped my elbows. I shrugged them loose and slowly picked up my bag and walked toward the ship. As I walked, I looked down at my feet. I watched as they moved me closer to the ship. With each step I stared at them, as if they belonged to someone else, or had a will of their own.

This isn't real, I thought. Someone will come forward. Papa will break the line. The Queen's man will declare me free. Somehow I'll be saved.

I started up the gangplank, hearing the creak of my shoes on the planks, hearing the pounding of my heart, the waves clapping the ship, the hiss of the engine, the squeal of the cables. Then, breaking above all else, I heard my mother's wail.

"*Auē!*" The sound of her grief.

"*Auē!*" The hymns.

"*Auē!*" The waves.

A chorus of mourning rose from the dock.

I ran to the ship's rail. "Mama!" I screamed.

Papa was holding her up. She was twisting and bending, forward and back. She reached out for me with her arms. Papa held her from behind. His eyes never left mine.

"Aloha, father," I whispered and kissed my hand and reached out as if I could touch him for one last time.

The *Mokoliʻi* set sail.

I stood at the rail staring at them, trying to burn the sight of their faces in my mind. I wanted to hold them, I wanted this all to go away. But the *Mokoliʻi* kept moving through the harbor, threading her way through tall ships and steamers.

My view of my parents was blocked. I ran up and down the rail trying to keep them in sight. I shoved my way through other patients. I craned my neck to see them.

Don't go away!

The wailing was lost in the sound of the ocean.

I stood at the rail staring at the pier. I never blinked. I squinted even in the dark. I stood there long after I couldn't see the dock, long after the ship rounded Lēʻahi and set course toward the channel.

From the ship I saw the fishermen's torches. They glittered on the waves, like stars that landed in the ocean.

What's going to happen to me? I thought.

I walked the deck to the farthest deck chair and covered myself with a blanket. I curled up as tight as I could and shoved some of the blanket in my mouth so no one would hear me cry.

What's going to happen to me?

I felt someone sit down beside me. I felt the weight of a hand on my shoulder.

"Don't worry," I heard a man's voice say. He rubbed my back and slowly lifted the blanket and tucked it under my chin. It was an old Hawaiian man. "It will be all right."

His forehead caught the light of the moon. He had a broad, square head. His ears were large and wrinkled and drooped lower than any I had ever seen.

"It will be all right," he said as he stroked my forehead. He was a dark-skinned man with kinky white hair that was cut close to his scalp.

"I'll watch out for you," he smiled. "And you can watch out for me."

I nodded and smiled back without thinking. I didn't know if I should be afraid of him. The man was barrel-chested and round-shouldered. The buttons on his shirt pulled open at his belly and the cuffs of his sleeves strained at his wrists.

"Look over there, boy," he pointed to a cluster of stars near the moon. "It's a good sign."

I didn't want to look at the stars or listen to some old man's lies. I didn't want to talk or smile. I wanted to cover myself up and be left alone.

The old man sat on the chair next to me, and I pulled my blanket over me and huddled under it with my back toward him. I laid awake all night, twisting and turning on the wooden chair.

What's going to happen to me?

I tried not to look at the sky for a sign, but more than once I looked up at the stars and begged the gods to show me.

By the time Io, the morning star, had risen, the *Mokoli`i* was moored off the coast of Kalaupapa and there still was no sign from the gods.

The ship's crew threw the nets off our baggage.

A *haole* officer barked his orders to a young deck hand, "E, Manu. Start with *tūtū's* bags." The officer wagged his fingers over a canvas trunk.

"Pikela, Manu, get the boats ready," he said. And the long boats were unlashed and lowered over the side.

The old man who had spoken to me slowly woke up. He stretched and groaned and pulled his suspenders over his shoulders. He looked over to me and nodded. I nodded back.

He lumbered to the rail, shifting his weight from side to side, resting his hands on his back. He took a place in a line of the young deck hands who were passing trunks, wooden chests, sewing machines, rocking chairs, beds, and baggage—from man to man into the dangling long boat.

I watched the old man as he lifted a chest of drawers. His fore-arms were thick. His skin was leathered from sun. He had no sign of disease. His face was clean and his body was strong.

He walked off the line toward an old woman and guided her to the railing. He took her by the waist. He spoke to her softly, smiling and nodding, then he lifted her into the long boat.

Women and children were boarded first. The women in long dresses tied their skirts to their waists and climbed over the rail. Some of them were wearing bonnets with lace nets that swirled over their faces. One woman was all in black—a wide-brimmed hat, her *holokū* trimmed with lace, and a parasol that hung from her arm. She leaned over to the two little girls who stood in front of her and whispered to them and kissed the tops of their heads. The girls, still clutching their dolls, climbed into the longboat by themselves

It was my time to board. I climbed into the third boat with the

men. I sat behind a crewman about my age. The old man sat next to me.

The *Mokoli`i's* crew lowered our boat. The rope slacked and there was a drop. The boat dangled—then a second drop bounced me off my seat. I scraped my back against the plank as I slid to the floor. The boat rocked, tossing me against the sides.

"Release!" a crewman shouted.

"Release," a boatman answered.

The long boat dipped. There was a third drop. Hot jolts of pain surged up my spine. The boat swayed.

"Release," was the call.

"Release ropes."

I got back on to my seat. The boat dropped and we plummeted into a wave. Water crashed in and the crewman in front of me was thrown into my lap. He grabbed on to my legs. My ribs slammed against the side of the boat. There was another swell and the boat pitched.

"Stroke!"

The crewman tried to climb back to his seat.

"Stroke!"

Another swell hurled the boat.

"Stroke!"

The crewman grabbed for his oar. The boat lurched into the break. We were caught in the curl of the wave. Water hissed and spewed.

"Stroke!"

We were surrounded by water. The crewman dug his oar deep. Waves slashed my face. My clothes were drenched. Crewmen were yelling. Oars collided.

"Stroke!"

Another wave came toward us.

"Stroke!"

It spewed us out broadside.

"Stroke!"

The boat pitched and reeled.

"Now!" a crewman yelled.

We careened up and plunged into the crest. The boat was righted and we rode out the wave. The yelling stopped, the strokes of the crew began to slow down, and soon there was order.

We survived, I thought. We survived.

With each stroke we moved closer to Kalaupapa. I could almost make out the landing. It looked like a small village in the shadow of the mountains. The Moloka`i cliffs rose out of the ocean like a thunderous wall of jagged ravines and cloud-covered peaks.

With every wave we lunged forward, stroke by stroke, closer to Moloka`i—*Moloka`i, a hina.* Moloka`i, the gray. Moloka`i of the dead. Kalawao, the land of living corpses, the land with no law, the place to die. Its spirit reached out for me. It came out of the mist. It sought me out and choked my breath. It chilled me and covered me. It brought with it the stench of death—my death.

I'm going to die!

It seized my soul and surrounded my body. I wrapped my arms around my shoulders and dug my fingers into my bones. I rocked back and forth and threw back my head.

Moloka`i of the abandoned!

I shut my eyes and rocked.

I'm going to die!

My mouth opened wide. I rocked faster.

"*Auē!*" I screamed.

"*Auē!*"

Water gushed over me in angry torrents.

Just let go, I thought. Let the ocean have you.

A wave flooded in.

Let go, just let go.

I dropped my arms and let the wave pitch me out of the boat. But I was pulled back, the old man grabbed me.

Let me go! I begged him, but the words never came out.

"Boy!" He pulled me back by my jacket.

Please, let me go.

"Boy!" He took me and cradled me in his arms.

"*Auē!*"

The old man rocked me.

"Auē!"

I cried out to Jehovah. I cursed him and begged him for mercy. I cried out for my father and mother. I cried out for Keo, I cried out to all the gods in the sky and asked them for their rescue. I cried until I couldn't cry anymore.

I sat huddled in the old man's arms, too weak to fight. I let him hold me and keep me safe as we drifted toward the landing. I kept my eyes closed, refusing to open them. If I kept my eyes closed I would be safe.

It worked until I heard the old man say, "Sit up, boy. It's time."

Chapter 2

The Landing

"Sit up, boy. It's time." The old man rubbed my back.

I didn't want to move.

"Get up, boy."

I opened my eyes.

Kalaupapa was straight ahead. To the left of the landing the surf sprayed ten feet above the cliff. The crewmen from the first boats were standing waist deep in water. They stood in a half-circle with their arms locked.

A wave lifted our boat and thrust us toward the jetty.

"Lean into it!" a crewman yelled.

The boat started to *huli*.

"Lean!" he yelled.

I held on to the side. My knees banged against the wooden ribs.

The boat dove forward. It rose, then sank, then there was a loud thud and a dragging sound of the bottom of the boat scraping sand. We landed.

A crewman helped me climb out of the boat. My clothes were heavy, dripping with seawater. They stuck to my skin and dragged me down when I tried to walk. I stepped lightly on each rock, watching my footing as I went. I took the hand of the first crewman, then the next, and so on through the chain of men guiding me over the jetty. I balanced myself holding their hands, while I kept my head down, watching for *puka*.

Each of my steps was cautious, and with each step another hand guided me. I fell only once, skinning my hands on the gravel. The landing had no path. There were only jagged stones and brown, pocked rocks crusted with moss and pea-sized mussels. The higher I climbed, the steeper the incline, but slowly I made it up, holding on to broken stumps and boosted up by the line of men.

When I made it to the clearing I looked up to say thanks to my guides. That was the first time I saw their faces—they had no faces.

These men who had led me, passing me up hand by hand, boosting me like luggage, guiding me like a dog—they were all misshapen! They were ghosts out of a madman's dreams or the conjured figures of the night. I was afraid to look at them. Their eyes had no life, their ears bulged, their faces oozed and swelled with tumors.

"Aloha," they welcomed me.

I wanted to run away, but there was no place to go. They were everywhere—hundreds of them were on the landing—almost all Hawaiian, some Chinese, a few *haole*. I never knew there were so many.

What's going to happen to me?

I couldn't look at them. I looked toward the sky, the ocean, the rise near the bay—there was a white clapboard building at the rise. It was the Board of Health station. Its sign, the paint peeling, swayed from chains. A small brass band was playing in front of the building. Over the sound of the wind I could barely make out the tune of a Queen Lili`uokalani song.

To the left of the building was a dirt field cluttered with buggies. Behind the buggies were the cliffs of Moloka`i rising straight up through the mist.

I staggered up the path to a reception line of *haole* men. They were all dressed in white suits and straw skimmers. I guessed that they were the doctors. One of them had a waxed red mustache. He smiled and leaned forward in a slight bow. The man next to him checked his pocket watch as I passed by. Most of them nodded at me and kept their hands clasped behind their backs. Not one of them reached out to shake my hand.

I looked down and picked the seaweed off my jacket. I saw my shadow, hunched over in the sand. I pulled my shoulders back and remembered all my mother's training, and I walked past them with the pride of a Ka`eo.

Next in line were the Catholic priests. They too were all *haole*, all dressed in black robes. Many of them had long, gray beards; most were bald. The Catholic sisters followed. The sisters smiled and bowed and kept their arms crossed with their hands tucked in their sleeves. They were all in habits. Veils and headpieces covered their hair and pinched their cheeks forward, making them look as if they had a permanent pucker.

The ministers and their wives were at the end of the line. They too smiled and nodded.

"Aloha," I heard from a voice in the crowd. "Anyone from Waimea aboard?" The voice came from the Board of Health building. There was a man standing on the verandah rail swinging from its post. He leaned out toward me. "Anyone know the Hee family from Waimea?" he yelled.

I stumbled over a rock and noticed that my hand was bleeding. Probably from the fall, I thought. My shoes seeped water and I could smell the seaweed stuck to my pants.

I walked toward the buggies. I counted fifteen buggies just in the circle in front of me, and what looked like hundreds of patients walked in the field or sat on mats.

I spotted the old man who had helped me on the *Mokoli`i*. He was in a far wagon. I started walking toward him when a *haole* man came up to me.

"Are you William Ka`ai?" he asked. He was about fifty years old. The man had a small, sharp face tucked behind a long, gray beard. His eyes were small, and he wore wire-rimmed spectacles halfway down his nose.

"I am William Alaloa Ka`ai," I said.

The man's work clothes were faded and his boots were so dusty they looked gray.

"I'm Dutton," he said, and shook my hand. He touched me, and he didn't seem afraid. "I'm here to take you to Baldwin Home," he said. "It's about three miles down the road." He continued to talk as we walked in the direction of the Board of Health building.

I looked back toward the wagon. "If it's all right, sir, I'd like to see someone," I said. I wasn't sure if he would let me go, or what was going to happen.

I asked the *haole* again, almost pleading with him.

"Take your time. I'll wait here," he said.

I ran up to the old man's buggy, but when I got up to him I didn't know what to say. I reached up for his hand.

"Mahalo," I said. Thank you.

"`A `ole pilikia," he answered. It was no trouble.

"I'm sorry for . . . for . . . for the boat," I said.

The man bent down from the wagon and held my chin in his hand. "There's no need to ever mention it again."

"Will I ever see you here?" I asked him.

"I'm sure," he said.

"What's your name?" I asked.

"Sam." He smiled. "Samuel Moses Ho`okaumaha."

"I'm William Ka`ai."

"Ā hui hou, William," he said. Until we meet again.

Sam sat on the buckboard in a puddle of seawater made by his clothes.

"Ā hui hou," I answered and made my way back to the *haole.*

"Are you ready, William?" Dutton asked.

"Yes, sir," I answered.

Dutton wiped his eyeglasses with his handkerchief as he began telling me the history of Kalawao. As he talked we passed by people who bid me welcome with a wave or a smile. Some yelled out questions.

"Have you heard anything about Captain Wilcox?"

"No, nothing," I replied.

"Is there news from the Queen?"

"Nothing I know."

"Do you know the Lukela family from `Ewa?"

"No, I'm sorry. I don't."

"What about the Yen Hoy family from Honolulu?"

As Dutton and I walked on, the music of the band drowned out their questions. The band was a ragtag crew of crippled old men in uniforms as tattered as they were. There were four tubas, three bugles, two French horns, one trombone, and a snare drum. The parade drum had the faded seal of King Kamehameha V painted on it.

These men are so old, I thought, they probably can remember the King.

But the closer I got, the more I could see that these old men were not men at all—they were boys, like me, but their bodies were frail and their faces were distorted. Some had no mouth, only tight puckered o's, and their noses had sunk into their faces. Only the tuba player looked clean.

"Do you play an instrument, William?" Dutton waved to the boys and they returned his gesture with smiles and nods. The trumpeter bowed and added a trill to his playing when we walked by, and the drummer saluted us with his stick.

"No, sir," I answered. "But my brother, Keo, plays the piano."

"Do you want to learn? It's a good way to pass the time."

"No, thank you," I answered.

"Well, maybe there will be something else that will interest you," he said. "There's lots of work to be done."

From what I could see he was right about the work. Half the planks on the pier were rotting and there was a rusted-out lift dangling from a crane.

"There's my bag." I pointed to it in the pile.

I reached for it but Dutton put his hand over mine. "It's all right, William. I have it."

Dutton's face was deeply wrinkled, his glasses were thick, and he walked with a slight limp, his head in what seemed to be a permanent cock. He easily hoisted my bag onto the buggy. We both climbed up and started down the dirt road. "You'll be living at Baldwin Home with the other boys," he said.

"Are there many boys?" I asked.

"Yes, quite a few."

"Are there any my age?"

"Your age and younger," he said. "You'll live there until you turn eighteen, then you'll move to the bachelors' quarters."

As we rode down the dirt road there were calls of welcome from people sitting on their verandahs. A woman tending her garden waved to Dutton and asked him about a boy named Jonah. When he told her the boy had died, the woman crossed herself and kissed her fingers the way that Catholics do.

Two cottages down there was a man rocking in his hammock. A sleeping cat was curled on his chest.

Across the road from him was a woman in a blue *mu'umu'u* sweeping the steps of her cottage. "How are you Brother?" She waved the broom in the air.

"Blessed by God with another glorious day," he answered.

The road was lined with white plantation houses. They were small clapboard cottages with two front windows and covered verandahs. Some were bordered with hedges of hibiscus or bougainvillea. Wild sweet grass grew in the yards and honeysuckle vines sprawled over the rock walls that lined the road.

As we rode by, Dutton told me who lived in each house. There was Ah Nee the tailor, Keola the poi maker, Lopes the saddle maker, and Mrs. Nahulu the teacher. "That's Ah Choy's house," he said, pointing to a dilapidated shanty on the mountain side of the road. "Hopefully, this time Ah Choy will let one of the men who came in today live with him. The superintendent is trying to get him a companion."

"Do you think my friend Sam will be assigned there?"

"I don't know," he said. "If Sam has any family or friends here he'll probably want to live with them," Dutton explained. "That's why so many people turn out at the landing. They're looking for friends they knew from before."

"What if Sam doesn't know anyone here?"

"Then the superintendent will place him," Dutton said. "But, even if he does get assigned to Ah Choy, that doesn't mean he'll live there. So far, Ah Choy has refused to allow anyone in his cottage."

We were coming up to the only yellow-painted cottage in the compound. At the cottage's path to the road there was a bougainvillea-covered trellis over the gate. "That's Makana's cottage," Dutton said. "Makana is a widowed *kōkua*."

"A *kōkua?*" I asked.

"Sometimes a person who is clean comes to the settlement to live with a patient—a *kōkua*," he said.

The woman was cutting flowers in her front garden.

"After her husband died Makana stayed on at Kalaupapa. Now she takes care of two men in her cottage by herself."

The woman pushed her hair back and wiped the sweat from her brow. "Hello, Brother." She waved.

He waved back to her. "Makana needs a strong man, and a good man, to help her with those two."

"Sam is a good man," I said.

"He'd need the patience of Job to live with the two she cares for."

Dutton brushed the flies from his beard. "The building up ahead is the Church of the Healing Water."

My eyes were getting heavy. I hadn't slept for two days, and as Dutton continued to talk his voice lulled me to sleep.

Dutton was still reciting the church's history when the jerk of the buggy startled me awake. The road was caked with mud ruts and covered with manure.

"That's Saint Philomena's church." He pointed to a building on the ocean side of the road. It had a tall square steeple, a clapboard side, some narrow colored windows, and some large windows with plain glass. There were curlicue arches, a fancy side door, and a wrought-iron gate that swung from an orange rusted hinge.

"Father Damien built that church," Dutton said.

It looked like it was made from spare parts each having nothing to do with the other.

Dutton slowed the carriage and we turned onto a narrow path toward the mountain side of the road. I caught myself sleeping, jerking my chin up before it hit my chest. I remember seeing the coconut-lined path. I remember trying to force my eyes open. There was the smell of a smoked fish, and I thought I smelled pig, but I may have imagined it or dreamed it. My eyes kept closing and my head dropped to my chest.

"William, we're here." Dutton nudged my shoulder. We stopped in front of a long white clapboard building that was part of a compound. Most of the buildings looked alike—long white buildings with verandahs that faced an open rectangular field.

I followed Dutton into the building. It was one big room, long and narrow with beds lining the walls. Dutton slid my trunk under the fourth bed on the right. He folded my jacket over the chair next to my dresser and left me to get some rest.

I don't remember falling asleep, I don't know how long I was asleep or how I woke up. It was either Paka who woke me, or it was the screams of boys playing with dogs.

The first time I woke at Baldwin Home I wasn't sure where I was. I was just coming out of my dream. I was in that safe place between wake and sleep where there is no trouble. I opened my eyes slowly and examined the room like an outsider. I went over each detail and tried to remember it, like I was going to describe it to my friends when I got back to Honolulu.

The room was all white—white walls, white ceiling, white trim on the windows, and white-painted doors. Seven beds were lined up against each wall. Each bed had mosquito netting hanging over it, and there was a window and a dresser between each bed.

It was just before dinner when I woke. The sky was already gray and I remember the wind through the palms sounding like rain. I looked around again, searching for some clues to figure out where I was. I was in a place I didn't know. I didn't know the rules, didn't know what I was supposed to do or not do, or who I could or couldn't trust.

There was a dark figure at the door. It was a boy. I guessed him to be my age. He was taller than me and more muscular. He began to walk toward me, bouncing his hand on the iron footboard of each bed as he passed.

"Aloha," he said.

His eyes were narrow and his hair matted. His shirt was open to his waist.

I leaned up on my elbow. "Aloha."

"I'm Paka," he said.

Paka's pants were cut off at his knees. He had thick, round calves. His feet were wide and his toes were splayed.

His feet look like he's never worn shoes, I thought.

"From Wailuku." Paka stabbed his chest with his thumb.

I doubted if he ever went to school, and if he did, I was sure it wasn't a proper school that made you wear shoes.

"Brother Dutton told me to come get you for dinner," he said.

I sat up in bed and stretched.

"What's your name?" he asked.

"I'm William," I said.

Paka reared back his head and snorted. "William? What kind of *haole* name is that?"

"It's my Christian name. Why?"

"You got a Hawaiian name?"

"My name is William Maka`ike Alaloa Ka`ai of the Ka`eo line," I said with all the bearing that my mother had taught me.

Paka mocked me with a bow.

"You got plenty names, boy, but you still got the *lēpela* just like me," he said. "Where you from, William?"

"Honolulu," I answered.

I reached over for my shirt.

"You going to wear that shirt?" he asked.

"What's wrong with my shirt?"

"You got different clothes, boy?" Paka asked. "You know, like fishing clothes?"

"My family is sending me more clothes on the next ship," I said.

"I didn't ask you about more clothes," he said. "I asked about different clothes."

Paka rattled the footboard of my bed. "E, Prince Loa, you can't go around wearing those clothes. Someone might kill you for your money." He winked as he walked down to a bed three down from mine and dragged a trunk from underneath it. "I think I can find clothes for such a small shrimp like you," he said. He held up a pair of trousers, then he looked back at me and shook his head. "No, too big for the royal Ka`eo."

He picked up a calico shirt by the collar and spread out the sleeves. "Here." He threw it at me. "And maybe these." He tossed a pair of trousers. "Get dressed, your highness," he said. "I'll wait for you outside."

I stood up and looked at my reflection in the window.

I am a Ka`eo, I thought. Anyone can see it in my face. My eyes are round, deeply set—strong eyes, with shrouding brows. Eyes that see keenly—*Maka`ike.* Paka knows who my family is. He must.

But when I looked down at my body in Paka's clothes I felt small. His belt cinched my waist and his shirt fell past my hands. My arms were thin and my calves showed my bones. My *tūtū* used to say that I had legs like a rooster.

"E, boy. You ready yet?" Paka called from the verandah.

"I'm coming."

From the dormitory verandah I scanned the common courtyard. Red bicycles leaned against the banyan tree in the middle of the field and boys swung from its branches. On the far mountain side of the quadrangle were two mango trees shading the stables.

Paka was leaning against the porch post, chewing on a piece of long grass. "You look good, Loa." He aimed the grass strand at my face.

"Paka," I said, as we started down the steps, "can you call me William?"

He poked the grass in my chest. "William is a no class *haole* name," he said, emphasizing each syllable with another poke. "It's better you be called Loa here."

"Why should I?" I asked.

"Boy, you ask too many questions."

Paka eventually took me to supper but not by the direct route. First we went down the coconut trail, the one from Damien's church. On the way he pointed out Dutton's cottage to me. It was a two-story cottage in the far ocean corner of the quadrangle. There was a flagpole in his front yard where Paka said Dutton hoisted an American flag every day at dawn.

Two Catholic brothers were walking about ten yards ahead of us. One was short and fat, the other tall and lean. Paka pointed to the one on the left. "The fat one is Brother Luis. He's the cook and baker. The other one is Brother André. He's in charge of ordering things for the kitchen, the stable, and all sports. He's a good man, and he's a good rider, too."

"Do you ride with him?"

"I did once. We went up a trail to the topside of the island— way up, toward the valley." Paka pointed to a waterfall. "Way up, near that waterfall. Do you see the cave next to the waterfall?"

I shook my head no.

"Maybe you can see it better from the other side of the cemetery," he said.

The short brother held the gate off the ground as he pivoted it open.

Paka jumped the wall of the church cemetery. "Both of those brothers work for Dutton," Paka said. "Everybody at Baldwin Home works for Dutton."

I followed Paka into the cemetery. The ground was so caked and dried that my footstep cracked it.

"What kind of man is Dutton?" I asked.

"He's all right. Sometimes he acts like he's still in the army."

As we walked, Paka grazed the top of every headstone with his hand. "The old-timers say his wife made him crazy and he went off and got drunk and had every woman he saw. They say that's why he came to the settlement. He felt guilty."

"About what?" I asked.

" So much *panipani*," Paka said. "But here I heard he hasn't been with a woman for fifty years. At least no *panipani* that anybody here knows about." Paka stopped and turned to me. "He hates *panipani* now. If he catches you laying with a girl, even one time, he'll throw you out of the home. Even if he catches you with pictures, you'll be in big trouble."

We took a wide loop past Damien's grave and headed toward a shed at the back of the church. The shed had planks of planed wood leaning against it.

"What's that?" I asked.

"Nothing," Paka said.

"Is it a woodshop?" I asked. "I used to help my father do woodworking," I said.

"It's not a woodshop. Come on." Paka pulled at my shirt.

But I yanked loose from his hold and zigzagged through the graves toward the building. I cupped my hands at the window and looked inside. Inside were stacks of coffins in different stages of completion.

"I told you not to look." Paka came from behind and punched me, hard on my shoulder, staggering me toward the lumber.

"Come on," he said, walking toward the ocean. "Too many questions," I heard him muttering to himself.

I followed behind him, not saying a word.

He stopped and pointed to a rainbow at the top of the cliffs. "Forget the shed," he said. "Look at the rainbow."

The cliffs of Moloka`i encircled Kalawao. They rose straight up from the ocean in furled sheets of green, with black-ridged valleys and blue smoke clouds that curled their fog through the peaks.

Paka found a spot for us in a clearing at the edge of the cemetery. It was near the ocean cliff—the drop was twenty feet. He turned toward the mountains. "Can you see the cave now?" Paka asked.

I couldn't.

"I hope you're better at getting fish," he said. "Fishing is good here. That's my spot."

It was at the mouth of a stream, in the direction of Kalaupapa.

I looked out to the horizon toward O'ahu. It looked so far away—just a gray-blue cloud on the horizon. It was hard to believe that the day before I was there, standing on the dock, being held by my father. It was just one day ago.

Paka held on to the stump of an ironwood tree and slid down the cliff. He reached for something on the ground and came back with a *noni* branch in his teeth. "When you get boils," Paka said, "the *noni* will take away the pain." He handed me the branch. "Nobody knows about this plant. Most of it is past the crater."

"Thanks," I said.

Paka stood up and wiped his hands on his pants. "I'm hungry. You ready to eat?" he asked. "There's good food tonight—stew, poi, and sea biscuits with brown sugar."

We headed back to the compound, and Paka swung his arm around my shoulder and we walked into the dining hall for our first of many meals together.

We sat side by side on the dining hall's long wooden benches, passing big white bowls of food, and stuffing our pockets with biscuits.

Later that night, in the dormitory, Paka asked me, "You got any pictures?"

"What kind of pictures?" I said.

"*Panipani* kind."

I told him I had lots of them at home, but that I didn't bring any.

I didn't tell him I never even saw one.

Chapter 3

Life in The Settlement

The next morning I followed Paka again—past the flagpole in Dutton's front yard, past men sitting on Dutton's steps—past the taro farmer from Līhu`e, the Chinaman from Honolulu, the stevedore from Lahaina who had worked with Paka's uncle.

Paka knew them all. He knew where they were from and what they did now, who was sick, who was dying, and who was sleeping with his best friend's wife. I smiled as he introduced me. I tried holding my breath so I wouldn't have to breathe in their stink.

The screen door swung open. "Come in." Dutton waved us in.

"You are looking well, William." Dutton lowered his chin and examined me from over the tops of his wire-rimmed glasses.

I shimmied in sideways as far away from him as I could.

Dutton's office was a neat jam of glassed cabinets, wooden files, and piles of parcels wrapped in brown paper. His walls were covered with photos of kings and queens. There was an oval lithograph of Abraham Lincoln, maps of America and Europe, and a painting of a church.

"Sit," he said, pointing to two high-backed chairs in front of his desk. "Make yourselves comfortable while I get us some biscuits."

Among the photos and maps hung two wall clocks, a dried flower wreath, and a shelf with a statue of Jesus. In the middle of the floor was a row of black metal trunks, strapped and locked. Next to them was a wooden crate marked, "Return to vendor. All hats damaged," underlined three times.

A music box sat on his desk. Next to it were rosary beads. Behind his desk was a polished oak bookcase filled with ledgers, stacks of newspapers, worn leather books, and a box filled with dozens of eyeglasses. On the top ledge was a portrait of an old woman in a gold oval frame.

In the far corner was a standing desk with cubbyholes for mail, a black metal safe, and a step stool.

"I have a cousin in Wisconsin who sends me biscuits every month." Dutton's voice came from the back room.

"Look." Paka slapped my thigh. "Get 'em." He pointed his chin toward a box of chocolates on the top of the safe. "Go ahead."

"No."

"He never miss them."

"I said no."

I looked away from Paka and stared at the doorway to the kitchen. An American flag was draped on the door. It was tied in the middle at the top of the door jam, making a triangle for a tall man to walk under.

Dutton continued, "Usually about half the biscuits make it in one piece, but this parcel looks perfect."

"Loa." Paka slapped me again. "Get 'em now, before he comes back."

I blocked out his voice and matched the ticking of the clock to the swing of its pendulum.

"Here we are." Dutton came out of the kitchen holding a tray of biscuits and three glasses of milk. I moved the ledger to the safe to make room for the tray. Dutton slid the tray onto his desk. His body was in a constant lean—his shoulders cocked left and his head tilted right.

"William, get those chocolates while you're there," Dutton said, as he backed himself behind the desk.

I grabbed the gold foil box and put it down right in front of Paka, with a "you-see" look on my face.

"People send me things all the time. This week it seems like they all sent candy." Dutton held on to the desk as he lowered himself into his chair. "I don't eat candy as a rule, except for some butterscotch when someone sends it."

Dutton held up the plate of biscuits. We each reached for a biscuit. They were more like crackers than cake. They were flat and white with pierced holes on the top of them in the form of a star.

"William, how are you finding Baldwin Home so far?" Dutton asked.

"Fine, sir," I answered.

"I asked Paka to take care of you for a while." Dutton nodded toward Paka. "He can show you around and introduce you to other boys."

Paka's mouth and shirt were already sprayed with crumbs.

"Have you had the opportunity to meet many people yet?" he asked.

"Yes, sir, I have."

"Call him Brother." Paka's words spewed crumbs in the air.

"You can call me Mr. Dutton, if you prefer," he said. "Brother is what Father Damien called me."

"Thank you, Brother," I said, and reached for two biscuits before Paka ate them all.

"Has Paka told you about his job here?" Dutton asked.

I shook my head no.

"He checks our water pipes. It's quite an important job."

"I'm the Water Supply Superintendent." Paka grinned, showing his teeth all packed with thick white dough.

"He rides six miles a day checking the pipes for damage."

Dutton reached over for a biscuit. His skin was as thin as wet paper but shiny, like the inside of a shell. His hands were covered with light brown spots and bulging green veins.

"I think you may enjoy taking a job," Dutton said. "Is there anything in particular you like doing?"

I had never thought about work before. I had always planned on becoming a doctor. Papa told me I would study at Yale.

"What kind of work would I do?" I asked.

"He should be a banker," Paka laughed. "Look at him with those clothes. He should be the Baldwin Home banker."

"That's enough, Paka," Dutton said.

"It's a new suit," I said, turning to Dutton. "My father bought it for me for my Board of Health picture."

"They are fine clothes, William. I'm sure they'll serve you well."

Dutton turned to Paka. "Would you like to wait outside while I speak with William?"

"No, sir," Paka answered.

"Good." Dutton slid his eyeglasses up his nose. "Now, William, what about work."

"Is there a school?" I asked.

"Yes. Would you like to be a teacher?" he asked.

"I mean is there a school for me?" I asked.

"Not past the primary years," he said.

"What about working in the superintendent's office?" Paka said. "William could help him assign the new patients."

Dutton took off his glasses and wiped them with a soft gray cloth. "No, I don't think that would be appropriate."

"What about your reports?" Paka said. "He could write reports for you."

"William, I could use some help with my bookkeeping. Would you be interested in that?"

"Not really," I said.

"Then what about writing?" He pointed to piles of envelopes tied up in bundles with blue and white string. "People from all over the world write to me asking about Baldwin Home. They want to hear from boys like you. Would you like to write to people from

Europe and America and tell them about yourself?"

"I would rather not," I said.

"Well, take your time," Dutton said. "Paka can explain what jobs we have and you can think about what interests you."

"Brother Dutton, I do like to write. I just don't want to write letters."

"Well, then, what about the newspaper? We have a weekly Gazette," he said.

"What could I write about?"

I finally got a piece of biscuit in my mouth. It tasted sweet and crumbly, not at all like it looked.

"You could write about our boxing teams, or visits by officials from Honolulu. Or, as Paka suggested, you could help me write my reports to the Board of Health."

"That's a good job for him," Paka said. "William is smart, Brother. He writes better than most of the *haole* teachers, and his Hawaiian is perfect. He can do all your translations." Paka kicked me under the desk. "William is very smart, Brother. He reads all the time."

I looked over at Paka. How did he know what I could do?

"Is that true, William?"

"Yes, it is," I said.

Dutton swiveled his chair toward the bookcase and dug through a pile of books. "In that case, William, I think you would make an excellent choice." He shifted ledgers and moved around a pitted brass scale.

"Here," he said, handing me some books. "You may like reading these. The bottom one is about the Hawaiian kings and queens, and this one," he tapped the top book with his thumb, "is *The Lives of the Saints.*"

The Lives of the Saints had a frayed green ribbon sticking out from the bottom. All the books smelled of mildew.

Dutton reached over and took both my hands in his. "William," he said, "the first few weeks here may be very difficult. I find that some boys enjoy reading to get them through it."

After one day, I already understood what he was trying to

tell me.

"Will William write for the newspaper, Brother?" Paka asked.

"If he would like to," was the answer.

"He would like to," Paka answered for me.

"Would you like to answer for yourself now, William?"

I accepted the position and Paka accepted all the leftover biscuits and chocolates. On the way out Paka picked up a copy of the *Gazette*.

The screen door hadn't slammed behind us before Paka was working on his next scheme.

"Now, a horse," he said.

I didn't ask any questions. I was trying to hold my breath until we passed the men on the porch. They smelled like rotten potatoes that get lost behind the cupboard.

Paka stopped short and hit me on the chest with the paper. "You are now the official editor in chief of the *Gazette*."

We cut behind Dutton's cottage and made our rounds past the dining hall. The air was heavy with smoldering *kiawe* wood and the tang of crisp pigskin. Paka saw me stop and sniff the air and look around.

"There was a pig hunt last week. Benito Lopes died," Paka said.

"First we see Brother Hermann," Paka continued his muttering as he walked.

"Paka," I said.

"Then, maybe I could try Brother Marc," he went on.

"Paka." I grabbed his elbow. "How did you know I read and write English?"

He shrugged his shoulders. "A skinny boy like you, soft hands, nice clothes, you call everybody 'sir'—It's no big deal to figure that out. You can do those things I said, right?"

"Yes."

"So what's the problem?" He took off his hat and rolled the brim into a tight curl, then angled it at a steep angle over his ear. "It'll be good for you to work on the *Gazette*," he said.

"Why?" I asked.

"You get to see the superintendent's report before anybody else."

I didn't ask him why that was so important, or where we were going, or what he was planning—there were too many other things I needed to know first.

During those first few weeks there were so many things to figure out and so many things to get used to—like the constant wind off the bay, and the early setting of the sun, and the fact that everyone knew who I was and what I was doing and where I had been. There were no secrets at the settlement. Everybody knew everybody else's business, and there were too many people with too little to do.

A man yelled to us from a bachelors' dormitory window, "E, Paka, come see me. I got something for you."

"Later," Paka yelled back. "I got to see Brother Hermann now."

I followed Paka into the administration building.

"Don't talk to this Brother, don't tell him anything, don't even look at him unless you have to," Paka said.

The Brother was sitting behind a dark wooden desk. He was a *haole*. He had light green eyes, like the color of the ocean over a sandbar. Like Dutton, he had a beard, but his beard was black and curly and grew out sideways over his shoulders and down his chest to the top of the two flaming hearts that were sewn on his robe. This Brother was dressed like all the rest, covered from neck to ankle and wrist to wrist in a flowing black robe. Only Dutton wore denim pants and jacket.

The Brother looked up from writing in his ledger. "Yes, Paka. Can I help you?" he asked. He lifted his head only as high as he needed to see us above his glasses.

"*Aloha kakahiaka,* Brother Hermann." Paka wished him a good morning.

"Good morning to you, Paka." His voice was indifferent.

"This is my friend, William." Paka put his arm on my shoulder.

"Good morning, Brother," I said and bowed slightly.

He took off his glasses and let them swing between his fingers. "Welcome to the Baldwin Home," he said. He stared at my face, then my body, right down to my shoes.

Paka shoved me closer to his desk. "William is the new editor for the *Gazette*. Brother Dutton just appointed him."

"Really?" At close range the Brother's eyes didn't look like the ocean. They looked like shards of green glass.

I kept silent, amazed at the ease with which Paka could lie. It was a remarkable skill, one I didn't have.

"He can read and write Hawaiian and English," he said. "In Honolulu he read poetry for the Queen."

I began to like Paka's game and stared into this *haole's* scrutinizing eyes.

"The Queen said he was very good," Paka said.

I pulled back my shoulders and looked down at the Brother like it was he who was my servant.

"William, have you, in fact, been presented to the Queen?" he asked.

My eyes drifted behind the Brother's face. On the top ledge of the bookcase was a statue of the crucified Christ.

"Yes, I have," I said. "I've read at `Iolani Palace." I continued my lie, staring at my Savior, hoping he wouldn't strike me down dead.

Paka put his hands on the Brother's desk and leaned toward him. "William needs his own horse," he said. "Brother Dutton said so."

Brother Hermann backed away from Paka. His eyes never left me. "Why, pray tell, does a writer need a horse?" he asked.

"To report the goings on of the day," I said.

"Brother Dutton wants him to pick up the superintendent's log and Mother Marianne's reports, clinic orders, things like that," Paka said.

Brother Hermann looked at Paka, then back to me. Slowly, he lifted a tab of his ledger with his pinched fingers. "A horse," he said, as he lifted the pages with two hands.

"Let's see." He smoothed down the tabbed page and dragged his finger down the lines of writing. Then he stopped and tapped at a line without looking up. *"Niele,"* he said. "What is your full name, William?" he asked. His head was bent over the ledger.

"My name is William Maka`ike Alaloa Ka`ai," I said.

"All right, William, tell Mr. Holokai that Niele is yours."

"Thank you, Brother," Paka said, and the two of us were down the steps before the screen door slammed behind us.

We went straight to the stable. Paka introduced me to Mr. Holokai, the stable master, and his assistant, Lum Kup. I met Kenzo Higa, the blacksmith, Japanese, and the three boys who work for him—Solomon, about ten; Momaru, a hairy Japanese; and his friend Kemamo, who was about my age.

Each time Paka introduced me he said my name was Loa. And so from then on I was known at the settlement as Loa Ka`ai.

The boy, Solomon, caught me staring at his hands. His hands were as curled as a rooster's claw. He had a metal cuff around each forearm that was attached to a small spade just past his hands.

"Better for eat," he said, and pretended to shovel food in his mouth. "Good for scratching, too." He grinned and dug under his suspenders and scratched his back with the spade.

Mr. Holokai led Niele out. She was a tall old hag with a gray muzzle and rotten teeth. The first time I saw her I thought she probably had a bad temperament. In time I found out my instincts were right. Niele was slow, stubborn, and had an obstinate will of her own.

* * *

All too quickly, life at Kalawao fell into a pattern. I spent my mornings writing for the *Gazette* and afternoons I spent with Paka. About three times a week I rode the length of the water pipe with him and we inspected it for leaks. We always took the same route—two miles on the dirt road down to Kalaupapa, then a sharp left toward the cliffs at the *heiau*, then up to the crater cemetery where we would stop to eat lunch.

There was a weekly routine, too. On Sunday mornings we were required to attend church and on Wednesday afternoons there were clinic examinations. Paka and I could sneak past the priests at church, but neither of us ever made it past the sisters at the clinic.

On the first Monday of each month the steamships brought in fresh shipments of fruit and poi and mail from home. They also brought in more patients.

I only met the ship once, it was the day the *Mokoli`i* brought my second trunk from home. I emptied my dresser drawers, dumping my banker's clothes on the bed. I unstrapped the belts on the trunk and was surprised to see a thick manila envelope on top. The return address was from the photo shop on Front Street, Honolulu. I shoved it, and a note from my mother, under my pillow and emptied out my new clothes.

I folded up my "banker's suit" and smoothed the jacket with my hands. I carefully laid it at the bottom of my trunk along with the two unopened envelopes. I closed the lid and slid the locker under my bed.

Now I had decent clothes to ride in. I could wear my own clothes, riding my own horse—my own mule is more like it, I thought.

Niele was beyond training. When Paka and I rode together, Niele would stop wherever she wanted to. Her first stop was at the crest of the hill, about half a mile past Damien's church, where the rock wall met the fence of the Church of the Healing Water.

Mrs. Na`ope was usually sitting in the yard on her swing, mending clothes or writing letters. She kept a wicker basket next to her. It was filled with cakes for Paka and me and mountain apples for Niele.

Every day Paka and I took the cakes and thanked her. We rode the same trail, had the same conversation, had the same dogs bark at us. We waved to the same men and wondered about the same women. At first the routine was comfortable, but, quickly, the fear of boredom crept in. I had figured out too early that there were no surprises at Kalawao.

The biggest excitement was the day a bull got loose in front of Saint Philomena's.

About twenty *paniolo* were on their horses encircling the bull. The bull was charging the church's gate. The *paniolo* twirled their lassos, some horses reared, a few drunken cowboys were baiting the bull. They made horns out of their hands and leaned over, scraping their feet on the dusty road, pretending to charge. The bull snorted, a few women begged the men to stop.

There had been a funeral that morning. The food flowed and so did the liquor. The dead *paniolo* was considered to be the best cowboy in the settlement—and his title needed to be claimed. A few hours into the funeral one man challenged another to a lasso contest. Then a few more joined in for a roping contest. The challenges got riskier until one man dared any man to ride a bull right into the church of Father Damien. It was an empty threat, but when Mad Nehoa heard it, he let the bull loose.

I looked around at the leather-skinned men next to me in their fine-weave hats, smoking their cigars. Most wore red paisley bandannas.

A lot of people at the settlement tied scarfs around their necks. I used to think the women wore them because it was their style, or maybe to catch their sweat. It was Paka who told me they wore them to cover their breathing tubes.

Paka told me that *lēpela* can fill up the nose and throat and block the airway. "So they slit your throat and put a tube in it," he said.

I stared at the bandanna on the woman next to me. I was watching for any fluttering, waiting to see air being sucked in when she breathed. I was curious about how big the tube was, how she slept with it, and if food ever got clogged inside. I didn't care about the bull.

The sheriff and his deputy were at the crest of the hill. I knew there would be a fight and I didn't want to get in trouble.

"Paka, let's get out of here," I said.

"No, this is the best part."

"Let's go," I said.

"No."

"Come on," he said, and the two of us shimmied up a tree and stayed until Paka counted the bloody noses.

For the next week all Paka talked about was the bull. When we were at the crater having lunch, he would tell me the story, filling in every detail as if I hadn't been there. And every time he told the story, the bull got bigger, and we were closer. Then he started telling me how he fought off two deputies and got a slug in at the sheriff.

We were at the crater when I asked him about the breathing tubes.

"Does the doctor put it in?"

"No," Paka said. "They ask the poultry farmer to do it." He spit blood on the ground.

"Of course, the doctor does it," he said. "But it's easy. Once at the beach I saw a man slit his friend's throat with a fishing knife."

With one hand Paka felt for the bottom of his Adam's apple. With the other hand he measured two fingers above the notch in his collarbone. "Right here, in between." He sliced across his neck with his thumbnail. "That's where you cut."

My mind flashed a scene of a man slashing his friend's throat and his friend bleeding to death on the beach.

"It's easy," he said.

I was never sure if I should believe Paka. He made up stories. I'm not sure he knew when he was lying himself.

He would tell me about people in the settlement as we rode by them. He told me the *haole* man who lived in a cottage with lace curtains was a pimp from Honolulu who ran a brothel that was really owned by the King. And the man who slept in his hammock, with the cat curled on his chest, had murdered his wife's lover. He said the clinic doctor had syphilis and that his wife sent him away.

The first time we rode past Ah Choy's cottage he told me Ah Choy sold white babies to traders in Shanghai. Ah Choy's house looked like it had the *lēpela* itself. The roof sagged, weeds grew up through broken boards on the porch, and half the windowpanes were broken.

A few weeks after we started riding together Paka asked me if the superintendent was going to send Ah Choy to the hospital.

"No," I answered. "Ah Choy told the superintendent he wants to die alone in his own house, with nobody watching."

"What else did the superintendent say?" Paka asked.

"He said he was going to force Ah Choy to accept a live-in helper."

As we rode past I tried looking in the cracked windows.

"Cha!" Paka said. "No one can live in that house." He spit cloudy phlegm. "That place stinks so bad your head aches as soon as you walk in."

"What kind of smell?" I asked.

"Sandalwood, opium, *lēpela.*"

I shaded my eyes from the sun and squinted to get a glimpse of the Chinaman inside but I couldn't see inside. The glare of the sun turned the dirt on the windows into a thick gray shield.

"Have you ever been inside?" I asked.

"Maybe I have, maybe I haven't," he said.

"Then how do you know what it smells like?"

"I just know," he said.

"How?"

Paka jerked his horse to a halt. "Sometimes, Prince Loa, you ask too many questions." His face was unsmiling.

"I just want to know," I said.

"Some things are better you don't know," he said.

"Why not?"

"Because you wouldn't understand," he said.

Paka rode leading the way. I didn't try to catch up. I rode the rest of the morning listening to the barking dogs and the soaring birds and the waves crashing in the bay.

When we stopped at the crater for lunch, Paka took his handkerchief out of his back pocket, and in a grand sweeping gesture he laid it on the ground and smoothed it out with his hands. Then he stood up and bowed. "For your royal *ōkole*, Prince Loa," he said.

I didn't think he was funny. I didn't move.

"Well, your highness?" he said.

I just stared at him.

"Loa, I'm sorry." He opened his hand and gestured for me to sit across from him.

I did.

He offered me some dried squid from his pail.

"No, thank you," I said.

"Have some crackers," he said.

"I have my own."

Paka clenched the squid between his teeth and tore a piece off with a tug of his head. "Maybe we can go fishing tonight," he said. "There's a full moon. Mahina blesses us." Pieces of squid sputtered out of his mouth as he spoke.

"I don't feel like going fishing," I said.

"Too bad," he said, wiping his chin with his hand. "I feel luck is with me."

"Paka," I said deliberately, "how do you know Ah Choy's house stinks?"

"I've been inside," he said, "at night when the old man was sleeping." He flushed the squid down with a gulp of water.

"Why?"

"I wanted to see what was inside. That's all." He shrugged his shoulders.

"The truth, Paka," I said.

"All right! I wanted to see what I could steal, that's the truth. Sometimes I go in the cottages—after the people go to the hospital or die—and I take things." He put his water jug down on the ground. "I took a chance going in Ah Choy's house. I figured he would be so full of opium he would never know I was there."

I leaned back on my mat and ate all my lunch.

"Paka," I asked, "is that why you want to know about the super-intendent's report all the time? So I would tell you what cottages are empty?"

Paka laughed. "Niele. You are getting to be just like her." He raised his chin toward Niele. Her name meant nosy or curious. "Niele Loa," he laughed louder.

I hated when he made fun of me.

"Yes, that's why I ask you about the reports," Paka said.

I didn't say anything.

"I don't take big stuff, just stuff I never saw before," he said. "Besides, what can the dead do with anything?"

"That's why you wanted me to work at the *Gazette*, isn't it?"

He started packing up his lunch pail. "What's your problem? It's a good job, it's easy and you get to pretend you're the royal poet."

"And you get your information."

"We both get what we want."

We each packed up our lunches not saying a word. But on the way home Paka tried to make conversation. He told me *lēpela* jokes and *panipani* stories. He asked me about my friends in Honolulu, about my family and my school. He even asked me about the books Dutton gave me about the kings and queens.

"Any stuff about Princess Ruth?" he asked.

"Yes," I said.

"And Kalākaua?"

"Yes."

"Did it say he owned brothels?"

"No."

When he asked me about Sam Ho`okaumaha I said I didn't know anything.

I didn't want to tell him anything about Sam.

Chapter 4

Supper at Makana's Cottage

It wasn't until the second week at the settlement that I found Sam.

The superintendent's report said he was "assigned to Building Number 244, a cottage owned by *kōkua* Makana Malo." It also listed patients Enrico Cabral and Kamaka Alexander A'ai as living there.

Makana's was the fourth cottage past the Church of the Healing Water, on the ocean side of the road, the yellow cottage. The windows and doors were trimmed in white and hanging baskets of mint and nasturtium swung from the verandah.

I noticed Makana one day on one of my rides with Paka. She was sitting under the mango tree in her front yard. Some girls from Bishop Home dressed in their red *mu'umu'u* were sitting on *lauhala* mats in a half circle in front of her. The girls were crouched around a bucket of water, splashing each other as they wrung out their leaves and giggling as they quickly took aim at each other.

Makana sat cross-legged in front of them, wearing a dark brown *mu`umu`u* that stretched taut across her knees.

"*Aloha `oukou.*" Good afternoon, I said, as I walked across the yard.

"Aloha," Makana answered.

Makana's hair was tucked behind her ears. It flowed down past her shoulders, curving around her breasts and curling in to two wide sweeps on her lap.

"Come." She motioned me forward with her hand. Her face was full and clean. She had a broad nose and full lips.

"Come," she said. Her eyes held the peace of Jehovah.

I stood at the edge of the mat with my hands at my side. "I'm William Ka`ai," I said. "I'm called Loa." As I explained who I was, the girls huddled together giggling even more.

Makana told me that Sam was marketing down at Kalaupapa. As she spoke, she pulled long strands of *hala* out of the bucket and squeezed the water out between her fingers. She told me to come back later for dinner. "Bring your friend if you'd like," she said, and waved to Paka who was waiting at the road.

I knew I wasn't going to ask him.

"Loa, before you go could you carry this *lauhala* to the lanai, please."

At the edge of the mat were rolls of dried *hala* leaves tied in two-foot bundles. When I returned for dinner that night they were still on the porch.

As Niele crested the hill that night I could see Sam in the distance, hunched over the fence. I waved, but he didn't see me. The sun had already gone down and the gray of Moloka`i had already settled in.

When I got there Sam hugged me, and I remembered the feel of his arms on the boat.

"Good to see you, boy," he said. He looked older than I remembered him to be. His face had deep wrinkles that started at his eyes and ended down past his cheeks. As we walked to the cottage, Sam rested his hand on my shoulder. He was walking with a limp.

"Are you all right?" I asked, pointing to his leg.

"Just a boil on my foot. Nothing really," he said.

"E komo mai, e `ai," Makana called from the porch. Welcome. Come into my house and eat. She was wiping her hands on her apron. "Come in," she said and hugged me at the door.

It was then that I realized I was at Makana's house as a guest and I didn't bring a gift. *"O na maka wale no keia i hele mai nei,"* I said to her. Only the eyes have come.

"I'm sorry," I said. "My mother would bring gifts when we visited. I'm sorry."

"Loa, we're blessed just to have you come," she said.

Sam walked toward the back door. "I'll go get Rico," he said to her.

"Thank you," she said, and turned to me. "I hope you like pie, Loa."

"I could smell it from the road." I smiled.

"It's mountain apple pie," she said. "And I have sweet potato pie and leftover venison from the Burial Society meeting."

Makana ushered me toward a rocking chair in the left corner of the room. "But, I need to get back to the kitchen and finish up Mr. A`ai's food, so you just make yourself at home. Sam will be right in and Mr. A`ai should be finished dressing soon." She pointed to one of two closed doors.

The cottage had four rooms that I could see. The living area was a long room that went from the ocean to the mountain side of the cottage. To the left, as you faced the ocean, were two closed doors. To the right was the kitchen.

In the middle of the living room was a dining table covered with a white lace cloth. The table was set with white china plates, blue goblets, and a spray of pink bougainvillea in a green glass vase.

In the far right corner was a steamer trunk. Above it, about four feet up, was a plate rail that held cups and saucers commemorating the coronations of Queen Emma and of King Kalākaua. From a row of pegs below the rail hung a straw hat with a black band and white

letters reading *"Aloha `Āina"* and a blue wool shawl.

In the opposite corner, to the left of the back door, there was a koa rocking chair and a small side table. On the table was a glass oil lamp, a Bible, a Honolulu newspaper, and a white pitcher filled with purple bougainvillea. On the wall just above the table was a framed photo of two men. One was Captain Wilcox, of the Hawaiian Patriotic League. The other man I didn't know. The stranger was tall. He had on a formal black jacket, white trousers, and a flowered vest that was crisscrossed with a watch chain. There was a crested medal pinned to his lapel. He posed with his hand on his hip.

"That's Captain Wilcox," the hoarse voice of the man behind me said.

I turned to see the man I assumed to be Mr. A`ai. "Yes, I know," I said.

"And that handsome fellow with him is me," he said.

I looked at the photo again. The man in the picture was heavy, he had clean skin, a full mouth, and his nose flared arrogantly over a full mustache.

"I've lost some weight since then." He laughed.

His eyes were strong in the photo, but now they were clouded over. His eyebrows were gone and his cheeks were pocked. The only resemblance left to the man in the photo was his dark, wavy hair.

The man leaned on his cane and, with a pivot, he lowered himself into the chair. "I am Kamaka A`ai," he said.

"My name is Loa," I said.

"Sam tells me you're from Honolulu."

"Nu`uanu Valley, near Kuakini," I said.

The back door of the cottage swung open hard, slamming against the wall. A stocky white-haired man with a bushy white mustache stepped just inside the door.

"What does your father do, Loa?" Mr. A`ai asked me.

"He's a teacher," I said.

"What does he teach?"

The man at the back door stamped his wet feet. *"Jesus Cristo,* A`ai, who are you? The Board of Health inspector? Who cares what his father does?" He started to walk toward me, wiping his hands on his bare chest.

He shook my hand. "Glad to meet you, Loa."

"Are you Mr. Cabral?"

"My father is Mr. Cabral." He grinned. One of his teeth was capped with gold. "Call me Rico," he said. He smelled of sweat.

"Rico," I repeated.

He pinched my waist and lifted my arm and felt my ribs. "You're a skinny one," he said. "I've got two daughters bigger than you."

Rico turned toward the kitchen. "Makana, are you cooking yet? This boy needs some good Portuguese food to fatten him up."

"I know you can smell food, old man," her voice came from the kitchen. "I'm making apple pie, just for you," she said.

"Good food ruined by the stench of you," Mr. A`ai said to Rico. "Why don't you wash? You smell worse then the *lēpela*."

Rico leaned over and tousled A`ai's hair. "You're just jealous, Hawaiian. You wish you had a body like mine." Rico's chest was brown from the sun and spotted white from the *lēpela*.

"Loa, go in my room and get my clothes off the bed." Rico pointed to the room where Mr. A`ai had come out.

It was easy to see which side of the room was Rico's. There were two beds, one covered with a patchwork quilt. Rosary beads hung from the bedpost. Over the bed was a picture of Jesus with arrows piercing his heart. On the bed table next to it were a faded wedding portrait and a recent photo of a plantation store—Cabral & Sons. At the entrance of the store was a woman wearing a sweeping peaked hat that was tied down with a scarf. There were five children crowded together on the steps.

"You making the clothes, boy?" I heard Rico's voice.

"No, sir," I answered.

I delivered the clothes to Rico and he went out to take a bath. By the time the five of us sat down to eat, an hour had passed already.

Mr. A`ai was seated at the head of the table, Rico was to his right, and I sat next to Rico. Sam was across from me and Makana sat opposite Mr. A`ai at the seat closest to the kitchen.

Sam said the grace, Rico passed the fish, and Mr. A`ai ate his rice and milk. Sam talked about the new recreation center that was supposed to be built at Kalaupapa. Mr. A`ai said it would never happen. Makana bragged about the Bishop Home girls learning to weave.

I said nothing. Rico was quiet, too, until he asked Mr. A`ai why he was eating only rice and milk.

"My stomach is no good," Mr. A`ai shook his head. "I was up all night with a vision."

"What vision?" Rico asked.

"Death," he answered.

"A`ai," Sam cocked his head toward me, "maybe we can hear this later, A`ai."

But A`ai continued. "Last night a warrior came to me in my dreams. He was wearing a loincloth, dyed red. And the left side of his body, from the top of his head to the soles of his feet, was black with a tattoo." Mr. A`ai traced a line down the front of his face and chest with the blade of his knife.

"The warrior walked toward the cottage." As A`ai spoke, his hands trembled and swords of light flashed off his knife.

"The warrior had a feral pig on a leash." His voice got louder. "The pig got bigger and bigger until it was so big I could see his eyes from my bed. The pig's eyes glowed orange, yellow, and black, like lava flow. And then, . . . " A`ai pointed his knife toward the road, "when the warrior reached our cottage he unleashed the pig."

A`ai leaned back and paused.

"And then what?" Rico asked.

A`ai sat with his eyes closed.

"A`ai, then what happened?" Rico got louder.

"And then I awoke."

"So what does it mean?" Rico asked.

"It means that death is coming. I have seen it," Mr. A`ai said.

"A blind man could see death in this place," Rico said.

"But death stopped here. In this cottage!" Mr. A`ai banged his fist on the table. "It came here!"

"If death is coming to this cottage, old man, we all know it's coming for you first." Rico laughed.

A`ai jumped up. He plunged his knife toward Rico's chest. "Fool!" he shouted.

Sam dove across the table. He grabbed A`ai's wrist and banged it on the table. He twisted the knife out of his hand.

The vase toppled over, and water soaked the lace. No one moved. The only sound was the water dripping onto the floor.

"Sit down, A`ai," Sam said softly.

Makana righted the vase and began blotting up the water.

A`ai dropped his head and began to cry. "I'm sorry," he said. "Makana . . . look what I have done to your beautiful table."

I slid my chair on the bare wood and got up to help A`ai. He was gripping the table's edge. His chest was heaving and his breath was foul. I picked up his cane and leaned it against the table. And while Sam and Makana moved the food, I cleaned up around A`ai.

"You're the fool, A`ai," Rico said. "I could have taken that knife and killed you with it."

Sam darted his finger at Rico. "Listen, old man. No more talk from you tonight. Not one more word. Do you understand me?" He thrust his finger into Rico's chest.

"It's all right, Sam." Makana touched Sam's arm. "It's over."

"Rico," Makana said, "whether it is your Madonna, or Jehovah, or a warrior spirit who speaks to us, we must listen to their voices. And in my house we will listen to each other."

"God forgive me," Rico said.

"Rico, Mr. A`ai." She looked at one, then the other. "I will have peace in my house, or you both leave."

"I'm sorry," Rico said to no one in particular. "It's the *lēpela*. It makes me act like . . . "

". . . an ass," A`ai said.

"I'm sorry," Rico said.

Mr. A`ai adjusted the lapels of his jacket and fluffed his neck scarf. "It's not the *lēpela*, it's you," he said.

Rico ignored A`ai and continued talking. "I, too, have a vision," he said. "I'm at the crater watching a burial. My back is to the ocean, but I can still see the water behind me. I feel like I'm floating over the settlement, and I can see far over the horizon past Kaua`i. Then my vision narrows—I focus on the coffin, it's mahogany. I see the faces of the children—Sandro, Jose, Maria, Caesar, Johana—all lined up at the grave. My wife is there too— pregnant with a son. The priest is sprinkling holy water on my coffin and the altar boy is swinging the incense burner. The prayers and the smoke rise and I am buried deep in the ground." As he spoke his tears fell to the table.

"And then all I see is my gravestone. It's a carved stone cross." Rico looked at A`ai. "I know my children won't be at my grave. And my wife has no money for a headstone."

He closed his eyes and was quiet. Tears trickled down his cheeks. "But I ask you, please," he clutched my arm, "bury my body deep." He opened his eyes and looked at Sam. "Deep enough so the dogs won't get me."

Sam nodded.

We returned to our meal slowly and ate our pie sitting outside on the verandah. When it was time for me to leave, Sam walked me to the road. The light of the moon turned his hair into a head of silver corkscrews.

"Sometimes Rico doesn't think when he talks. He says whatever comes into his head," Sam said.

"Is it really the *lēpela* that makes him like that?" I asked.

Sam smiled. "Part of it, maybe," he said. "But I think A`ai is right. Rico's probably been that way all his life. Did he scare you?"

"No, he didn't scare me . . . well . . . "

"Well what?"

"I didn't think old people were afraid to die," I said.

Sam smiled. "Do you think I'm old?"

I did, but I didn't say.

"We're all afraid to die, Loa," he said.

"You, too?"

"I'm more afraid of the *lēpela* than I am of dying. Do you understand that?"

"Yes." I already understood what he meant.

"But it doesn't stop me from living." Sam ran his fingers through my hair and cupped his hands around my cheeks. "It makes me live stronger. I live and I work . . . it's what I know how to do."

Chapter 5

The Plan

The first steamship in May brought a shipment of stilts, kites, bicycles, baseballs and bats, a box of Japanese glass marbles, boxing gloves, and a new parade drum for the band.

From my desk in Dutton's office I heard the crack of a bat squarely hit a ball. A loud cheer followed, then a thud against Dutton's wall and the grumbling of the men playing cards on his verandah. I poked my head out the window.

Dutton slowly made it out to the porch. "Yes. I will speak to the boys." He put his hand on one of the men's shoulder. "Yes, yes," Dutton agreed. "They should be more careful."

Dutton motioned for the boys to come to him. He ordered them to pick up the tables and chairs and gather up all the cards. Some boys chased cards that were tumbling in the wind, scooping them up in the grass. Other boys haphazardly righted the chairs as they mumbled an ordered apology.

Dutton assured the men that if such an incident happened again, he would take the bats and balls away. Then the boys got back to their game, the men back to their cards, and Dutton came back into the office.

"Are you a baseball player, William?" he asked me.

"No, sir. I like fishing and riding," I said, as the two of us lifted a heavy box onto his desk.

Dutton scored the box with his pocket knife. "When I was a boy I enjoyed freshwater fishing," he said.

The box was packed with crumpled-up sheets of the *New York Daily Tribune.*

"As soon as the lake thawed, I was out with my fishing pole." When Dutton leaned over, his beard covered the top of the box.

I pulled out the newspaper to uncover a box of candy. There were butterscotch and licorice, pink mint candy and sugared red peanuts, red-hot cinnamons and a soft candy wrapped in wax paper that Dutton said was saltwater taffy.

I had never seen so much candy. It was certainly enough for all of us, I thought.

But Dutton scratched his head and went off to the kitchen. "Not enough," he said. I heard him opening cabinets and slamming drawers. "William, try a piece of saltwater taffy," he called from the kitchen.

It was overly sweet and jammed in my teeth. It tasted like *mochi* that had gone bad.

"Here." Dutton handed me some brown paper bags. "There should be about three bags here. I want you to walk around and give out candy to the younger boys," he said. "No more than five pieces each."

When I was ready to leave, his voice stopped me at the door. "William, no more than five pieces for each boy."

I went straight to the dormitory and dumped almost all of the candy in my trunk. I left about twenty pieces in one of the bags, grabbed my fishing pole and tackle box, and headed straight for the stables to see if Paka could go fishing. He said he would meet me as soon as he finished grooming his horse.

I took a shortcut to the beach, through the coconut grove across from Damien's church. I waved to a few boys on the way but I didn't give them any candy.

When I crossed the road I saw a boy sitting with his back against the church wall. His knees were spread apart and his head hung down between them. His feet were clawed around the walkway. He was tracing lines in the dirt with a twig that was as mangled as his hands.

"Aloha," I said. "You want some candy?"

He looked up and smiled.

I felt my eyes bulge and my breathing stop. I tried to speak but nothing came out. The boy's face was gone, replaced by bulging black tumors and shiny stretched skin that oozed with pus. His mouth was no more than a wrinkled slit, and his eyes, or what were left of them, looked swollen shut.

My God.

I heard myself pant. The boy turned his face away from me. I squatted down where I stood and placed the bag of candy in the dirt. I gave it a slight kick toward him, then I walked past him, hoping he wouldn't speak.

I walked with my eyes straight ahead, staring at the ocean. I walked as fast as I could without running, then, when I turned the corner of the church, I ran. I ran through the cemetery, past the coffin house, past the grave markers, on to the gravel, then on the sand and I took off my shoes. I ran over the rocks—all pocked and black, all bulging with shells and crusted with foam. I tore off my shirt and pulled off my trousers. I stood naked and raised my clenched fists. I thrust my arms to the sky and began to wail.

"Auē! Auē!"

I looked toward the heavens for a sign from my God.

"Damn, you," I yelled. "You don't care."

I held my face to the sun—I wanted it to burn the *lēpela* from my skin—to burn me clean—to have the salt sting the disease from me, to have the wind scrape me smooth.

"Burn," I cried. "Oh, God, let me burn."

I felt the heat pierce my skin. My sweat crawled on my face, like hundreds of ants eating off the poison. I could see the red of the sun through my closed eyes, and I could smell the bitter salt in the air. I unclenched my fist and let my arms fall to my sides.

"Damn, you," I said. "Why did you let this happen to me?"

I opened my eyes slowly. The waves pounded the rock, smoothing the lava to a glistening shine. I could hear the sound of my own breathing—the wheezing had begun.

"Where are you, Oh God?" I screamed. *"`Aukea la i kou pono?"* Where is your justice?

The sting of the salt filled my nose, the sound of a frigate bird—the screech of its call, the flap of its wings—the men in canoes fishing off the coast, the horses in the pastures, the clouds over the mountains. This was my life at Kalawao.

I sat at the edge of the tide pool cradling my knees in my arms. I rested my chin on my knees and watched the fish swimming in a frenzy, groping for the smallest bit of water.

"Damn you," I whispered.

"E! Loa!" I heard Paka call. "You went swimming already?"

"Not yet." I turned my face away from him and wiped the tears from my face.

Paka laid down his bait and poles and took off his clothes. The *lēpela* marked a white stripe across his chest and down his thighs. The stripe almost covered his legs. Paka looked down at his chest. "I can't pass for clean anymore," he laughed.

"You couldn't fool an inspector."

Board of Health inspectors came around to our houses and schools and places where people worked. They lined up students at school and stevedores on the dock and examined us all as "suspects."

I rubbed my cheek, now smooth and clean. It was my cheek, a little red rash that suddenly appeared and just as quickly disappeared, that betrayed me.

"How did they get you?" I asked Paka.

"My neighbor, a Japanee man, turned me in." Paka's eyes, narrow for a Hawaiian, turned hard. "He got three dollars from the bounty hunter."

Paka baited his hook. "I was ten years old when the bounty hunter came for me. He put me in handcuffs and took me to Lahaina for a test."

Paka put down the hooks and rocked on his ankles. "The doctor put a needle in my foot. The needle had a long wire attached to a battery box. He flipped a switch on the box, but I felt nothing, not even the needle. Then he put the needle here." He pointed to his calf. "Nothing. Another doctor came in, all covered with gloves and a mask. He pushed harder. I felt pressure but no pain."

I looked at my own feet, bleeding from the rocks. I could barely feel them.

"My father wanted to kill the Japanee," Paka said. "But my mother stopped him. She didn't want him to go to jail. That was seven years ago."

"Did your father kill him?"

"No, and I'm glad. I want him to get the *lēpela* and come here so I can kill him myself." Then it was Paka who wiped tears from his face.

"Who turned you in?" he asked.

"My teacher," I said. "He came to my house one night and talked to my father, quiet like. I thought I was in trouble in school."

"The next morning my father and I went to the doctor. He scraped some skin off my cheek, where I had the rash. That was a Friday. I stayed home from school all the next week. I had to stay in the house, so I thought I was being punished." As I spoke I tossed smooth pebbles into the water. "The next Friday my father and I took the trolley car to Honolulu. He bought me a new suit—my banker suit." I looked up at Paka and smiled.

"In the afternoon we met Mama and my brother, Keo, at the photography shop. We all had our picture taken together. Then I took one all by myself. That's when I knew." I reached over for the hooks. "Three days later I was here."

"Do you have the photograph with your family?"

"It's in my trunk."

Paka and I went back to our fishing, and we sat telling each other stories and eating candy.

Paka sat facing the mountains. "You see that waterfall?" He pointed to a trickling flow over the cliff. "There's a cave just to the right of it. It's a lava tube," he said. "I found it when I went riding with the Brother. You see it?"

I cupped my hand over my eyes, but I couldn't make it out.

"It's where I hide my stuff," he said.

"What stuff?"

"The stuff I steal from the cottages—for when I escape."

I stood up to cast my line. "So you're going to escape?"

"You don't believe me."

I shrugged.

"I'm going to go to Pelekunu." He pointed to the valley at the mouth of the bay. "There's a whole settlement of us there—those of us with the courage to leave this place."

The beach at Kalawao was like a cove. The ocean mountains poked out of the water and Mōkapu Island floated on the water like a Portuguese sweetbread. To its right, just offshore, was the tall, sharp triangle of Ōkala Island. It was close enough for a strong swimmer to get to—a lot of the men rowed out there to fish. The mouth of Pelekunu Valley was right there.

"The streams are filled with shrimp," Paka said, "and taro grows wild."

It was at the mouth of Pelekunu Valley where the mountains, the ocean, and the sky came together. A constant mist rolled out of the valley. A`ai said it was "the white luminescence of roaming spirits that are calling our souls to join them."

I had heard stories about patients who escaped to Pelekunu by climbing the *pali* or by taking canoes around the spit. I knew it was Pelekunu where the first patients fled to seek shelter from the rain and cold of Kalawao.

"Do you know anybody who has escaped?" I asked Paka.

"No," he said, "but Lum Kup does."

"How are you going to live?" I asked.

"I have a plan."

"What about the sheriff? He'll track you down."

"I have a gun . . . I have three guns," he said.

"They'll hunt you with dogs."

"I'm not leaving until the dry season. Then I'll zigzag up the cliff and mark false trails for the dogs to follow."

"They'll still keep coming," I said.

"I got it figured out—I bait the trails with pork. But first I rub it with opium." Paka laughed. "When the dogs eat it, they'll get so confused they'll loose the scent."

"It won't stop them."

"Maybe," he answered.

I pointed to the "mark of Kāne" on his cheek. "And that? How are you going to escape that?" The black scab on his cheek was edged with raw skin.

He squatted down to bait his hook.

"What are you going to gain?" I asked.

"My freedom," he said. Paka's voice was weaker than it was a month before. He was constantly spitting, and most of the time his spittle was mixed with blood.

"You don't believe I'm going to do it, do you?" he asked.

"I believe you," I said, not particularly being truthful.

"Do you want to come with me?" he asked.

"I'd have to think about it," I said.

"Prince Loa has to think. You just decide! Come," he said.

"I don't know."

"You'll want to go after you've been here a while, but then it will be too late. I'll be gone."

"When are you going?" I asked.

"The end of June, on the full moon. The rainy season will be over by then."

On the walk home I looked for the trail going up to the falls, but I couldn't see it.

That night at dinner I looked at the boys around me. Some looked clean, most didn't. As I looked at their faces I could trace the progress of the disease—the bulge of the eyebrows, the drooping eyelids, the blindness. With some of them the *lēpela* withered their

fingers, with others it swelled them. Some of them had hands covered with ringworm, others had skin peeling from their palms.

In time they all looked alike, they lost their faces—claimed by
lēpela, and finally there was nothing left of them but the mask of
the disease.

After dinner I walked back to Saint Philomena's church. I sat
under the pandanus tree near Father Damien's grave. The sun had
already set and the gray of the sky blended with the sea. Only the
land was lightened by hundreds of white crosses reflecting the
clouded moon. In the distance Pelekunu was a dark shadow.

I leaned against the tree with my knees apart, tossing pebbles at
stray cats. Do cats get the *lēpela*? I wondered. I picked up a mangled
twig and traced lines in the dirt. The cats looked untouched, I
thought. Free and clean. I've never seen a leprous cat.

The bells of Saint Philomena's called the priests and brothers to
evening prayer, and they filed into the church, oblivious of me.
Curls of incense rose out of the open windows, and when the men
began their chants I got up and went back to the dormitory.

Later that night I woke up and sat up in bed. I pulled back the
gray mosquito netting and looked at the rows of beds, all veiled
under the same ghostly tents. Twelve curled-up bodies of boys with
the disease. Not one of them would be alive in three years.

That's when I decided.

The next morning at breakfast I sat with Paka. "I'm going to
Pelekunu with you," I said.

* * *

From that morning on I did everything differently. When I read any
of Dutton's memos, I calculated what I could steal. If Dutton
ordered one box of bandages, I changed the number to four. If he
told me to requisition one shovel, I asked for two. When he told me
to inventory his medical supplies, I stuffed my pockets with rolls of
plasters and vials of liniments. I stole knives and forks from the
kitchen, ink from the print shop. I even stole from the dead.

In a letter Dutton wrote to Mrs. Mahiko he stated: "All of your husband's effects, the trunk, the hamper, the box, and all of the items on the memo attached, are being sent to you."

The memo listed $150 in gold coins. I rewrote the memo, changing the amount of gold to $50.

I talked to Paka about medical training. I knew that if we really were to escape one of us needed to get trained. I also knew Paka's attitude about studying, so I knew that the one of us would have to be me. My plan was to ask Brother Dutton to support me in becoming a hospital assistant. I presented my case to Dutton and got support from Mr. A`ai and Father Wendolin.

The following Monday I started work at the Kalaupapa hospital. It was mid May and the heavy rains should have passed, but the rains continued and the road to Kalaupapa was pure muck. Niele took the ride slowly. By the time I arrived at the hospital it was already two o'clock.

The branch hospital was on the promontory overlooking Kalaupapa. Behind it, on the far side of the bay, the cliffs curled to the right to meet the ocean. And beyond the cliffs, forty miles away, the island of O`ahu floated on the horizon.

The hospital was actually two long white clapboard buildings. Both the mountain and ocean side had a covered verandah. Eucalyptus and alligator pear trees lined the Kalawao side of the hospital, shielding it from the rain and wind. A white fence with chicken wire nailed to it surrounded the building. Another fence of barbed wire protected a vegetable garden from scavenging dogs and pigs.

The path from the road to the hospital was one big puddle. The reflection of the hospital's stilted buildings floated on the mud.

I tied up Niele and made my way up the steps. I was wearing my suit; it was wrinkled from being squashed in my trunk. I tugged at my sleeves and tried smoothing out the wrinkles as I walked by waiting patients. They were playing cards, strumming guitars, and cooling themselves with palmetto leaf fans.

The ceiling of the verandah was painted blue, and pots of sweet-smelling mint hung from the beams. The windows shone without a streak, and the door handles were highly polished brass.

I opened the door and was hit by smells of camphor, iodine, tobacco, and potted roses.

Along the walls were lines of high-backed chairs filled with round-shouldered patients. In front of them, sitting on stools, were men who I guessed were the physician assistants. They were almost all men in the early stages of the disease, dressed in white shirts with armbands with a medical sign embroidered on them in red. They all wore black neck scarfs and dark blue aprons, and most had on gloves.

Between each patient was a wooden table. A woman in uniform was picking up the tin basins off the wooden tables. Another woman followed, putting down clean linen. A few others came out of a back room with white enamel pitchers of steaming water. They filled each of the basins. They all wore their hair piled high in a bun, showing off their high-collared blouses. On their sleeves they had the same red-embroidered armbands. They all had on black skirts that fit tightly at the waist.

A young girl, maybe sixteen, came in from the mountain-side door. She wore a black fitted skirt and a high-collared blouse, but her hair was down—tied at the back of her head with a wide black bow that hung midway down her back. Her hair was the color of a pheasant, `ehu-colored hair that flared wildly at the sides and flamed red in the sun's rays.

She saw me watching her.

"Aloha," I said.

Her face broke into a wide grin. "Aloha." Her eyes were dark almonds.

"May I help you?" one of the Catholic nuns asked me. The nun was tall, even for a man. She was dressed in a black robe that was tied at her waist with a rope.

"May I help you?" she repeated. Her face was fair and her eyes were light. She wore a black veil over a headpiece that looked like a white cotton helmet. The headpiece flared into a white bib that covered her chest. The cloth around her cheeks was wet with sweat but the nun still smelled like sweet lavender.

"I'm William Ka`ai," I said. "Brother Dutton sent me to be

trained as a physician's assistant."

She unfolded her arms and shook my hand. "I'm Sister Augustine." She wore no gloves.

"Kamalani," the nun turned to the girl, "get one of the men to help you take those bandages out to the boiler."

The nun turned back to me. "How old are you, William?" She guided me by my shoulders past the line of patients.

"Almost sixteen," I said.

We walked to the back room. "Brother Dutton must think highly of you to send such a young man."

We entered a doctor's office. Kamalani followed us in. She walked behind the sister toward a basket of soiled bandages. As she left the room she turned to me and smiled.

The doctor's office was at the mountain corner of the building. It was a dark room. The walls were lined with glassed cabinets filled with leather-bound books and jars filled with milky potions.

The doctor came in. He was a short, straight-backed man who smelled of snuff. He had the look of a man who never dreamed. He sat in his chair, pulled off his gloves, and folded his hands on his desk.

Sister Augustine began to introduce me. "This is William . . . "

The doctor waved his hand in the air and rolled his words over hers. "I understand you are here to assist at the hospital," he said.

"Yes," I said.

He took a gold filigree box out of his vest pocket. "Do you have any skills?" He opened the box and pinched some snuff under his long *haole* nose.

"I need to be trained," I said. "But I learn quickly."

Mo`o pupuka, I thought. You ugly lizard.

"You can begin by helping Kamalani," he said. "She can train you to inventory our stock."

"I'm here to train to be a physician's assistant," I said.

"You will train to take stock and deal with bandages first," he said.

"I know how to count, and I'm not here to stoke an incinerator. I'm here to be trained as a physician's assistant."

"Arrogance won't win me." He pushed his chair from his desk.

"I studied chemistry and physics at O`ahu College. Before I was sent here I planned to study medicine at Yale, like my two uncles before me. I am not here to win you over. I'm here to make the best use of my talent." I met the doctor's eyes, challenging him to question me.

Paka would have been proud of me, that I could lie with such ease. I had only seen O`ahu College on our Sunday rides on our way to picnics, and as for my uncles, they were both farmers.

"Who is your uncle?" he asked.

"Dr. Peter Trumbull," I said, remembering the name of a doctor who lived next door to mama's sister, on Liliha Street.

"A good man," the doctor nodded. "All right. I'll give you a two-week trial," he said. "Sister Augustine, see to it that the boy is an apprentice to `Ōpūnui." He started out the door but stopped to come back for his cane.

It's true, I thought. These doctors don't touch us. They just lift our clothes with their canes and prod us like cattle.

"Thank you, doctor," Sister Augustine said.

The doctor walked out without answering her.

"You handled yourself quite well, William. Mother would have been quite proud," she said.

These *haole* women were so strange. Paka told me they were all virgins. They said they were married to their God. They called each other Sister and the eldest they called Mother. They all lived at Kalaupapa without any men, while the men lived in Kalawao without any women.

Sister Augustine introduced me to `Ōpūnui, who was the chief medical assistant. `Ōpūnui was a Hawaiian from Waimea. He was a sturdy man, light skinned, with bristly white hair that spiked out in darts from his head and his beard.

"Sit down, William." He pulled a stool next to his.

"`*O Loa ko`u inoa.*" I'm called Loa, I said to him, as he helped a patient to her chair.

The patient was an old woman with an ulcer on the sole of her foot. The woman's *kōkua* stood behind her, resting her hands on the patient's shoulder. The *kōkua* explained to `Ōpūnui that the ulcer wouldn't heal.

"Come closer, Loa." `Ōpūnui lifted the woman's foot and turned it to expose the sore. "There are different ways to treat ulcers. There is the *haole* way and the way of the *kahuna*. I use both," he said softly.

`Ōpūnui put on his gloves and mask and proceeded to cut out the ulcer. While slicing the wound he spoke to the *kōkua* in Hawaiian. He told her how to use the noni plant—how to pick the best leaves and make the best poultice, how to mix it and how to apply it to the sore. He told the kōkua to keep the old woman out of the ocean until the next full moon and to have her put her feet up on a stool whenever she sat.

The second patient had dry throat. The *haole* doctor prescribed a green medicine. `Ōpūnui explained to the woman how to take it. Then he told her to chew the sap of the hau tree buds in order to loosen the tightness in her chest.

The next patient was a man with a fever, and after him was a woman whose husband had beaten her. As soon as one patient got up, another sat down. Most came to get their dressings changed.

The Catholic sisters did most of the dressing changes. They came in after their morning prayers and stayed until dinner. They took turns sitting on stools wrapping wounds, washing the sores of their patients, and offering the patients the comfort of their God.

From time to time Kamalani came by our table to restock our supplies. When she walked by, we both smiled.

"Pay attention, Loa." `Ōpūnui showed me the ulcerated mouth of a child. "Look here, not at the girl," he said.

I craned my neck to see inside the child's mouth. `Ōpūnui and I were almost cheek to cheek. "Loa, don't be so foolish. If the sisters think you're after Kamalani, your training will be over," he said.

I kept my eyes on the patients. Three hours passed. My head was throbbing and I felt nauseous. The sun had gone down and all the patients on the verandah had been treated.

I stood up to wash my hands and got dizzy. I grabbed the edge of the table and sat back down on the stool. `Ōpūnui wiped the sweat from my forehead. "I'm a little tired," I said.

"Loa, clinic work is not for everyone," he said. "There's no shame in not coming back."

I was determined to stand. "I'm coming back," I said.

"There's a lot to learn," he said, "and the patients never stop coming."

"I can learn," I said.

Sister Augustine dragged a stool next to mine. She sat with her legs apart, pushing her habit down between her knees to form a pocket.

"We made it through another day, `Ōpūnui." The nun lifted the rosary beads that dangled from her waist and placed them in her lap.

"Yes, Sister, we did," `Ōpūnui said.

"And you, William, you are going to be a great help to us," she said.

"I didn't do anything but watch." I felt embarrassed. I knew she had seen me falter and `Ōpūnui wiping my brow.

"You did fine," she said.

"I felt sick," I admitted.

"William, my first day here I lasted ten minutes. I was in panic. I felt like I was being smothered by disease. I almost ran out of the building," she said. She shook her head. "I couldn't eat for days. I gasped for air whenever I even passed the building. During the day I couldn't look at the patients, and at night I was afraid to sleep because of the nightmares."

She reached out and took my hand between hers. "It took me a week before I could get up enough courage to walk back in. That was four years ago," she said. "William, there still are days when it is only the grace of God that gives me the strength to serve the sick. Believe me, son, you will be of invaluable service."

"Thank you," was all I could say.

She slapped me on the back. "What about dinner, William? I know Brother Luis has closed up his kitchen already. How are you going to eat supper on these nights?"

"If you could ask Brother Dutton for permission for me to miss dining hall meals on these nights I could eat at a friend's cottage."

If she got permission for me, I could have three nights of freedom, I thought. I could meet Paka and we could plan our escape.

"Consider it done," she said, and she grabbed a basket of soiled linen and went on to the next station.

`Ōpūnui invited me to his cottage for dinner, but I said no. All I wanted to do was to go back to the dormitory and sleep.

On Monday, Wednesday, and Friday I went to the hospital after working at the *Gazette*. On Tuesday and Thursday I rode with Paka to the crater. Once a week we went up to the cave.

* * *

The day after my sixteenth birthday we went to the cave. My knapsack was especially heavy with a throw net I had found on the beach. It had rained heavily the night before, and the trail up to the cave was slick.

Paka went up ahead of me. He always had to be faster and stronger. He had to be the better climber, the better fisherman, the fiercest hunter. It was true, Paka was strong and sure-footed, and I was slow and cautious.

Some of the trail got washed out. Some turns were so narrow that I flattened myself like a crab with my belly against the rock as I inched along the ledge. Sometimes I would loose my footing, and more than once I slipped on the clay.

I pictured Paka going along, not even testing his next step. I was trying to speed up my pace, to catch up, when the ledge gave way. I heard the dirt beneath me break and I could feel myself slide. I told myself to move slowly. I clawed at the cliffs with unfeeling hands and grabbed for a tree root. It held.

My face was scraped against the rock and my knapsack was weighing me down. I swung my leg around the ledge, straddling the spine of the cliff. The tree root snapped. I slid down, rocks bounced against the mountain. I grabbed for plants, grass, the smallest ledge.

I'm going to die.

I dropped into snapping branches, hoping they would hold as I heard them crack and break. I tumbled onto a solid branch, safe, then I shimmied down the tree.

"Paka!" I called out as loudly as I could.

I had fallen about twelve feet.

"Paka!"

I knew he could hear me. It was so quiet I could hear the distant roar of the waterfall.

"Paka!"

He didn't answer.

I looked around and tried to figure out how to get back up to the trail. There was a stream to my left, and I decided to follow it. I thought it probably started at our waterfall and I would just get to it by a different route.

My knapsack cut into my shoulders. My chest was sore from the fall, and the mud sucked at my shoes and I had to lift my boot high. I was tired and had to cheer myself on. And with every turn I said to myself, "Just a few more feet. You can make it."

There was a wide ledge that cut deep into the mountain, and with its trees and a small cave, it made a good resting spot. I sat, exhausted. I was angry at Paka. He enjoys making me feel like the weak one, I thought. Maybe he even watched me as I fell.

Paka thought he was the hunter and I was Prince Loa. He was the master planner, the plotter and schemer, and I was the King's companion.

"Paka!" I cried again, but I knew he wouldn't answer.

The trees on the cliff trapped the musky scent of *laua`e* fern. From inside the cave I could see sunlight splintering through the branches, making shafts of smoking clouds filled with whirling dust and bugs.

I forced myself to get up. I leaned over as I walked and walked straight into a spider web, breathing in its film. I wiped its silky threads off my face.

"Paka!" There was no answer. The only sounds were the twigs breaking under my feet and the distant waterfall.

The path began to widen and the sun streamed in. Around the bend in a clearing, sitting under a tree, was Paka.

"Didn't you hear me call you?"

"I heard you, I just couldn't tell where it was coming from." He grinned.

"Did you look for me?" I asked.

"I didn't want to get lost," he said.

"You could have called back," I said.

"You should have kept up," he said.

"The ledge gave out. There was a rock slide."

"Probably more like a foot slide!"

"I could have died," I said.

"You have to learn to survive," he said.

I tossed my knapsack and walked to the ledge at the end of the clearing. From the ledge I could see the entire settlement below me. The peninsula looked like a small spit of land sticking out into the ocean. How well the early Hawaiians named it—*Ka lau papa*, a flat-tongued leaf.

I could see the road from Kalawao to Kalaupapa. It looked like a dusty yellow line between the two settlements. In the middle of the peninsula I could see the bulging Kauhakō crater.

Kalaupapa was laid out like a plantation town, with stores and churches, cottages and stables, but its only crop was white wooden grave markers.

Paka came over to sit next to me. He let his legs dangle over the thousand-foot drop. I ate my lunch as we talked. Paka didn't eat, he didn't have much of an appetite lately and he was spitting up blood a lot.

There were times I suspected that he was going blind, but when we got up to hike the last leg of the trek, Paka took off without me. He almost danced across the trail while I probed each and every crevice.

The trail got steeper before it flattened out and looped back toward the cave. I took another rest before crossing the waterfall, content to have Paka go ahead. I laid my canteen down and noticed a light green shoot of a weed that had broken through the cliff. High on the *pali*, where survival was a struggle, this frail, pale flower dared to bloom.

When I got to the mouth of the cave, I heard Paka shout over the sound of the falls, "I thought you were dead, old woman."

The cave was dark and damp. Water dripped from the roof and moss grew on the walls. Our cache was lined up against the walls—guns, knives, tools, cooking equipment, medical supplies, beer, rum, salted fish, wooden casks, lanterns, gold, blankets, mats, matches, and two lockers.

"Let's see the fishing net," Paka said, and he took one end of it and walked it to the far side of the cave while I held the other.

"This is worthless. This isn't a net, it couldn't hold anything. It's all holes!" he said.

"It needs to be mended," I said.

"It's no good," he said, and tossed his end on the ground.

"You could learn how to fix it," I said.

"You learn," Paka said.

"I'm learning to be a doctor." I dragged my end of the net and folded it over his. "Rico could teach you how to fix it," I said.

"That stupid Pordagee hates me."

"Rico's all right. He'll show you how to make a net if I ask him."

"Why me? Your hands too good for work?"

"And who are you?" I said. "The great warrior?"

"I'm going to keep us alive!"

I folded up the net and laid it next to the guns.

"We need a net," he said.

"I'll find a net," I said, "and I'll learn how to fix it."

"Once we have a net we'll have everything," Paka said.

"I want some journals and pens," I said.

"What for, smart boy? You going to write a book?"

"I want to keep a journal."

"For what?" he asked.

"For when they find us," I said.

"If they find us they'll put us in jail," he said.

"No, I mean after—when we're dead."

"You know what, Prince Loa? I think you think too much."

I readied myself for the hike down. Paka was rifling through one of the lockers. He saw me watching him as he took out a handful of gold coins.

"It's to buy opium—for when the pain gets bad," he said.

Chapter 6

An Easy Meal

I finally brought Makana a gift, even if it was from Brother Dutton. An Italian baroness wrote to Dutton asking him what she could send the girls at Kalaupapa. He asked her for fabric to sew dresses for the girls. Six months later the baroness sent three lace tablecloths and a yellow porcelain vase.

When I arrived at the cottage Sam was in the front yard sitting on a stool sharpening his machete. Makana was sitting cross-legged on a *lauhala* mat next to him. She was braiding her hair with quick twists of her wrists, whipping black strands into the air.

"Aloha!" Sam called. "Come." He motioned me over with his machete. "You've come just in time to save me."

I leaned over to kiss Makana.

"Maybe you can talk some sense into this old goat," she said.

"Don't bother the boy, Makana. He's come to have some peace, not to hear an old woman nag."

"You watch your tongue with me, I'm not even close to old."

Makana was forty-one years old, my mother's age, but she looked much older. Her skin was weathered by the sun and her hands were callused by hard work.

"Sam, you work too hard and you know it," Makana said.

I leaned over to hug Sam.

Makana tossed her braid over her shoulder. "Father Wendolin wants Sam to supervise the gymnasium repairs." She sighed. "Whenever a bolt is loose or a roof leaks, Sam is the first one he calls. If the fence post rots he calls on Sam. The bath's not working? Sam! He knows the man won't refuse!" Makana directed her words at me.

Sam took a deep breath and exhaled with a loud sigh. "Makana, your cottage is never neglected. I tend to your repairs first." He pointed the machete to the vegetable garden with its white picket fence and barbed wire screening. "I help you with the yard, I take A`ai for his baths, I re-roofed your house, and soon you'll have a covered swing so you can sit and watch the ocean from your back yard. Don't worry about what I do for the Father."

He pointed the machete to his chest. "What I do with my own time is my own business."

"I just want you to relax and enjoy life," Makana said.

"I enjoy work," Sam said.

I laid my wrapped gift box on her mat and got a stool off the porch. I heard snoring coming from the front bedroom.

Makana moved my gift off the mat. "I've got to finish up cooking." She rolled up her mat, tucked it under her arm, and walked away, muttering every step of the way.

"Maybe she is right, Sam," I said. "Maybe you do work too hard." I set my stool down next to his.

"You, too, Loa? What do you want me to do? Sit around and wait to die?"

He pointed to the boiled peanuts in his tool box. "I've worked hard all my life. For a while I had my own farm, then I opened a carpenter's shop with my brothers." He put the machete down on the ground and was looking around. He turned to look behind him. "If I didn't work in this place I might as well be dead. *"O ka luakupapa`u kanu ola,"* he said. The grave of the living corpses.

I tossed a peanut in the air and caught it in my mouth.

Sam turned toward the porch. "Loa, go get me that can of oil."

The can was on the rain barrel under the kitchen window. Sam had cut a hole through the verandah roof and rigged a gutter pipe to catch a flow of fresh water in the barrel. Sam squeezed the oil can, snapping the metal. Oil dripped onto the sharpening stone, and he guided the blade over the whetting stone in slow careful circles.

"Do your brothers still have the carpenter shop?" I asked.

"They own it with my wife," he said. "Before I came to Moloka`i I divorced my wife, like the old style, and I gave her my share of the business."

In the old style, husbands and wives divorced each other, and children who were sent to the settlement were spoken of as dead. "It was better for the family left behind," the old-timers used to say. Mothers and fathers said they buried their child instead of admitting they had a child with *lēpela*. *Lēpela* brought shame. So families mourned and grieved and never mentioned the sick again.

In the old style, Catholic priests prayed over the bodies of the sick who would lie prone on the church floor. The ill were covered with a black cloak, and the songs of the dead were sung.

But the church thought that was cruel and after a while there was a change. With the change the diseased member sat in a chair facing the altar, blocked from the congregation by a black curtain. He could then sit and listen to the mourning, the prayers and the songs of the dead.

In the old style, *lēpela* marked entire families. Brothers and sisters of patients were automatically "suspects" and they were constantly tested for the disease. At school their playmates, who maybe once shared a bowl of poi or slept next to them on mats, were often forbidden from even speaking to them. Sometimes aunties who once showered us with kisses, grandparents who cherished us as their blood, would deny that we were related.

And in the old style, husbands divorced their wives so that the lives of the family would be better.

"My brother said business dropped down a little bit. But it's back up to what it was." Sam put the machete back in its sheaf and picked up a long-bladed knife.

"Can you show me how to sharpen a blade?" I asked.

"Come." He guided my hands under his, and with a slow, steady pressure he coaxed my hands into slow, smooth strokes. I couldn't feel the calluses on Sam's hands. Already the *lēpela* made my hands almost numb. But I could feel the pressure. The skin of Sam's hands was nicked with light scars and raised with bulging green veins.

"That's it, Loa. You got it." His voice was soft. "Keep the angle of the blade low." He pushed my wrist down with his thumb. "That's it. Slow." The skin of his knuckles was powdered gray.

He cupped his hands over mine, gliding the blade of the knife as it pushed the oil on the surface of the stone. Without realizing it, I lifted up on the blade.

"Don't lift. Just move . . . there . . . good."

I felt his rhythm in my hands and I sensed the angle of the edge.

"Good. Now the other side." He flipped the blade over. "Keep the edges even. You need the same pressure on each side. Good."

The oil turned cloudy and picked up black flecks from the blade.

My hands stopped resisting Sam's. He lifted his hands off mine and I guided the blade by myself, repeating Sam's pattern.

"Let's see what you did," Sam said, as he took the knife from me.

He held the knife close to his eyes, changing its angle to catch the rays of the setting sun. Then he held the tip to his nose and the handle out in front of him.

"See, no burrs," he said, and turned the knife toward me. "It's smooth."

Then he ran his thumb up from the base of the knife out to the tip, then flicked it over the honed edge in about eight places. "The best test it to feel the edge." He handed me the knife. "No snagging on your skin."

I took the knife and examined the edge. I repeated Sam's motion, examining it in the sun, looking at it straight on from the tip of my nose and running my finger up the blade. I was afraid that I would get cut.

"Sam," I had to admit, "I can't feel so much with my fingers." I couldn't feel the blade.

He cocked his head and took the blade back, then he felt the polished edge. He did it again and again, and each time he did it his smile got broader. Then he looked straight at me.

"Neither can I." He broke into a grin. "But I've been doing it like that for so long, in my mind I can still feel the blade." He laughed. "I wonder what else I only think I can do." He slapped me on my back. "At least I can still taste food! Come, let's go inside. If we're late for supper it will be more *pilikia* with Makana, and we'll all feel it!"

I wiped the stone with a rag, and I collected up the tools.

* * *

Makana waited until supper was over before she opened Dutton's gift at the table.

"This is lovely," she said, as she held up the tablecloth for all to see. "Loa, remind me to send some pie back to thank the Brother." She passed the cloth around for all of us to see.

Rico caressed the lace against his cheek and kissed the cloth like it was his lover. "Loa, you should give pretty things like this to your girlfriend." He jabbed me with his elbow. "She'd give you more than pie in return." He winked.

"Aya, Cabral, must you always think with your crotch?" Mr. A`ai took the cloth and held it up to the candlelight. "It's beautiful, Makana, and it suits your home well." Mr. A`ai gently folded the tablecloth and passed it to Sam.

"I heard your friend is a wonderful young girl. Her name is Kamalani. Is that right?" Mr. A`ai asked.

"Kamalani—Beloved Heaven," Sam said, as he walked over to the koa trunk and put the tablecloth inside.

"She's a doctor's daughter from Kāne`ohe," Mr. A`ai continued.

"A doctor's daughter?" Sam turned to Mr. A`ai.

"Sam," Makana said, "I was going to put that cloth in my dresser, not in the trunk."

"A doctor's daughter would make a good wife, don't you think?" Sam lowered the lid on the trunk, sliding the peg bolt closed.

"They say doctors' daughters know what makes a man's body feel good," Rico said.

"Leave the boy alone, Rico," Makana said.

"He's not a boy," Sam said. "He's a man."

"Young love! A moonlight ride to the crater and you can be in paradise," Rico said.

At night I had dreams of Kamalani and me going to the crater. The two of us would swim naked in the lake, or we would be lying on the grass. In my dreams I felt her hand on my face and I drew her close to me as we kissed.

"Aya, men!" Makana threw her napkin on the table. "I am one woman in a house full of men!" She stood up to clear the dishes from the table.

Sam rubbed her arm as she collected the plates. "If Loa took a wife, we would have two women in the house."

Makana slapped his hand.

"Two women in one house! No house should have two women."

Rico crossed himself. "I pray the mercy of God spare me that pain."

"I pray to God, too, Rico," Makana said, "to spare me from you and your constant foolish words." Makana gathered plates and went to the kitchen.

"May our young people perpetuate the race." Mr. A`ai raised his beer glass toward me in a toast. Sam and Rico joined him.

"I hope the boy is better at perpetuating the race than your kings," Rico said. "All they do is spill seed in their laps." He wiped beer foam from his mustache with the back of his hand.

"What would you have them do? Breed like sows for your

pope?" A`ai replied.

"The pope is a holy man," Rico began his defense.

I was tired of Sam and A`ai bickering and haggling and pecking at each other like old roosters too weak for hens. I picked up some plates and brought them into the kitchen.

Makana was at the counter slicing *pōpolo* berry pie. She wiped the knife on her apron after cutting each slice, just like my mother used to do. She was humming while she worked and didn't notice me at first. It sounded like a melody my mother used to sing. I remembered falling asleep in my mother's lap, feeling the sound of her voice vibrate in her chest and the cool of the tradewinds brushing my skin.

I remembered Sunday picnics in Nu`uanu, swinging from banyan vines flying over the stream. My brother, Keo, had just learned to clap. I climbed the tree and dove into the water just to make him clap over and over again.

"Loa," Makana turned to me, "could you ask Sam to help Mr. A`ai to the verandah. We can have our pie out there."

I remembered my mother baking pies, not blackberry *pōpolo* pie but mountain apple and mango. I remembered walking home from school and turning the corner smelling pies fresh baked, hoping the smell came from my house.

I went out to give Sam the message and returned to the kitchen.

I remembered long rides to `Ewa to visit my cousins. We rode past the Chinamen, waist deep in muck, tied to their water buffalo as they plodded through the paddies.

"Do you ever miss O`ahu?" I asked Makana.

She lined up five plates. "Not often. What about you? Do you think about home much?"

"I try not to," I said.

The pie crumbled as she scooped each piece onto a plate.

"Do you write to your family?" she asked.

"I haven't yet."

"Oh, Loa." She turned toward me. "They probably would like to hear from you."

"Brother André writes to them every week about me."

"You know it's not the same."

On clear days I could see O'ahu from Makana's back yard. It looked like a blue-gray mound on the horizon that could have easily passed for a cloud. The view was better from Kauhakō crater. I could see the slope of Makapu'u and I imagined the red clay of the *pali*. Sometimes I would stare at the island and imagine I could see Keo rolling a ball to Mama in our front yard or Mama taking him to the dry goods store. If it were Sunday I would imagine them on a picnic or visiting Tūtū Malia. On Tuesday night I knew Papa was teaching Bible class.

I imagined them walking down Maunakea Street, stopping at the Chinese bakery for sugar pineapple and moon cakes, leaving with a stack of boxes tied with blue string. I could hear the rusted bell clang when they opened the door. Papa would hold the door open with his back, moving sideways for more customers to come in.

I imagined them meeting people they knew on the street, stopping to exchange pleasantries, never mentioning my name, then continuing on their way, stepping around the lei makers sitting on the sidewalk with baskets of flowers for sale. I imagined them strolling past the corner of Front Street and King, where Davis Photography was, where we had our picture taken.

I wanted to write to them, but what could I say? How could I tell them I wanted to come home or that I wanted everything to go back like it was? What's the use of saying things I knew couldn't be?

"Would you mind if I wrote a letter to them?" Makana asked, as she straightened the collar of my shirt and lifted it by the seams on my shoulders. "I could let them know that you are in good health and well taken care of."

I kept my hands at my sides and stared at the floor.

"I can tell them about your friends, about your job at the hospital and how you are loved by a woman who has no son of her own." She lifted my chin and I raised my eyes to hers.

"He aloha 'oe na'u , e hi'ipoi nei." She hugged me. You are love for me to cherish.

Makana turned to the counter and handed me two plates of pie. "Here, take these out to the men."

I put A`ai's plate on the lid of the water barrel next to the rocker and set Rico's on the porch rail, next to his favorite cane-back chair. Sam and I ate on the verandah steps. My back was against the hedge of thorny bougainvillea.

Makana kicked the screen door open. She had a plate in one hand and a hanging lantern in the other. "Sam, why don't you sit in a chair?" She motioned toward the one next to Rico.

"I'm content here," Sam said.

"But you would be more comfortable on a chair," Makana said.

"I'm fine here," he said.

"It would be better for your legs not to sit all cramped up," Makana said.

"She nags you like a wife," Rico said. "Why don't you just marry her and get some benefit at night?"

Sam dug his fork into his pie.

"*E, nei,* remember Hokela Holt's wedding?" Mr. A`ai said.

Rico sighed. "Ah, good food, dancing all night, *machete* and mandolin music, beautiful ladies." He kissed his fingers. "It was a good night."

"Sam, you put the tablecloth in the trunk, didn't you?" Makana asked.

A rider stopped at the cottage and tied his horse next to Niele.

"I wanted it in my dresser," she said.

I tried to make out the figure in the dark. It was Paka.

"We need another wedding like that," Rico said.

"Aloha ahiahi." Paka greeted us all good evening.

"Aloha," Sam and Mr. A`ai answered.

"Paka, you're just in time for pie," Makana said.

"Thank you, Makana," he said.

"What brings you here?" Rico asked.

"Brother André sent me to get Loa. There is a new boy who is asking for him."

There isn't any new boy, I thought.

"He's been crying for him."

Makana went in to get Paka's pie.

"Which boy?" I asked.

"You know the young one from Honolulu. He knows your cousin."

"Oh yes, Imiola," I said, nodding my head. "Is he still upset?" I asked.

"Yes," Paka said. "Brother André thinks you can help."

"Then we should go back now," I said, wanting Paka to get stuck in his own trap.

"I'm sure he can wait until I finish my pie."

"No, I think we should go now," I said.

"Makana," I yelled into the kitchen, "Paka has no time for pie now . . . "

"Wait, Loa, I could put it in a basket for him and the Brother," Makana said.

"We can't, Makana. I'll come back for Dutton's pie tomorrow, after the *Gazette*." I hugged Sam, Rico, and A`ai and said my good night, and by that time Makana was at the door.

"Come after lunch tomorrow," she said. "I'll be at the girls' home in the morning."

I kissed Makana and we left. Paka and I mounted our horses.

"I wanted pie," Paka said.

"You're the one who said we had to get back to the dormitory right away." I mocked some tears. "Off to see that poor new boy." I turned to Paka. "Why did you come out here?"

"We're going to Ah Choy's tonight. I arranged to buy opium," he said.

"What do you need me for? If you want to survive, you have to survive on your own. Isn't that what you say?"

"Shut up," Paka said. "You wouldn't have the guts to make the deal."

I didn't blame Paka for not wanting to go to the cottage alone. Rico said it was filled with ghosts that moaned in the night. We rode up to the cottage slowly. Neither of us dismounted.

"You go in first," Paka said.

"All right," I said, figuring I could stall. I struck a match to light the lantern. Each time I held the match into the wind so it would go out.

"You got that thing lit yet?" Paka whispered.

"Not yet."

Paka started walking up the path. Once he was on the verandah, I followed. I heard the scurry of what I hoped were mice.

"Rico said there are ghosts in this house," I said.

"Rico thinks the saints talk to him," Paka said. He opened the door slowly. "Ah Choy," Paka called. "Ah Choy, it's Paka."

"Ah Choy?" He inched his way in the dark.

I lifted my lantern above Paka's shoulders, lighting up the room. "Ah Choy?"

"Maybe he's dead," I said.

"So much the better. Then we can take anything we want." Paka stepped toward a pile of rags on the floor.

The house smelled of urine, incense, sweet opium, and *lēpela*. I put the lantern on the floor and tied my bandanna over my nose and mouth. I caught a whiff of feces as I leaned over to pick up the lantern. There he was. Ah Choy, sprawled on top of a long floor pillow. He was a languishing human form, all twisted in silk pajamas. He had a queue that snaked around his neck and a small head covered with a Chinaman's cap.

"Bien wai?" Who is it? His voice sounded like a death rattle.

"My name is Paka. I'm a friend of Akiona Spencer," Paka said.

"Yup loy. Yup loy." Come in.

I pictured the stench of his feces filling my lungs.

"I want buy opium," Paka said.

"You want opium?" Ah Choy dragged himself up on his elbow. "You got gold?"

"I got," Paka said.

The room was filled with statues of Buddha and bowls of smoking incense. Ah Choy leaned toward a low table and reached for a long-stemmed pipe tipped with filigreed silver.

"You have fifty dollar?" Ah Choy asked. "I give you one bag for fifty dollar."

"I have one hundred dollars," Paka answered. "You give three bag."

Ah Choy sat up and pinched off a corner piece of the brown gum opium. He rolled the gum between his thumb and finger.

"Two bags. No more," he said, as he stuffed the gum in the ceramic bowl of the pipe.

"Too much," Paka said.

Ah Choy held the blue and white bowl over the lamp's flame. A heavy scent sweetened the air. Ah Choy brought the pipe to his face, trying to find his mouth. Twice he poked at the wisps of his mustache before he found his lips.

"Two bags and half." Ah Choy sucked in deeply, leaning back with his first inhale.

"It's a deal," Paka said.

Once more Ah Choy put the pipe to his mouth and inhaled slowly. He drew in the smoke and held his breath for a long time, then he coughed out smoke, spittle, and blood.

I tucked my head in my neck like a turtle and turned away from the stench. Straight armed, I swung the lantern through the smoke. I stepped toward the wall covered with photos. One was of a man, a woman, and three children in high-collared Chinese dress. The other was of two men standing behind a grocery store counter. The older man was next to a cash register. There were small wooden boxes piled on the counter. A streamer with Chinese writing was nailed to the wall behind them. Next to it was a shelf of bananas and paper-wrapped cakes. Both of the men were smiling, both were wearing Chinamen's hats over long braided queues. Both were in long-sleeved shirts. The younger one was pointing to a wooden sign with carved-out Chinese writing. Behind him was a shelf of jumbled-up woks, chopsticks, dragon-painted soup bowls, and bamboo steamers.

"In there." Ah Choy pointed to a black lacquer box. He leaned back in a stupor, sprawled like a dead squid.

Paka ransacked the box. "You see anything you want?" Paka asked me.

"No, let's get out of here."

Ah Choy moaned.

Paka riffled through a red-painted desk and stuffed something in his shirt.

"I'm going," I said, trying to hold my breath until I made it out the door. I ran as fast as I could without breathing in the stink of the cottage, then I pulled off my bandanna and drew in clean night air—sweet with plumeria, ginger, and honeysuckle. I breathed in the ocean salt and took in the light of the moon. I wanted to fill myself with everything clean.

Paka slapped me with a heavy roll. "Here," he said, "now you've got paper for your journal."

He had stolen long sheets of paper that the Chinese use for drawings.

Chapter 7

Rico

The next day when I went back to Makana's there was no one in the cottage. The smell of fried eggs and sausage lingered in the kitchen and there was folded laundry on the dining table. I heard whistling coming from the back yard.

"Rico?" I opened the back screen door.

He was sitting in a high-backed chair that was flaking with dark green paint. He sat with his legs wide apart. His pants were half unbuttoned and his shirt was bunched up in his fly.

"Aquí." Here I am, he said, turning from working on his net.

"Aloha," I called out.

The fishing net was tied between two eucalyptus trees and billowed in the ocean breeze.

"Makana is still at the girls' home." He angled his netting needle through the holes and drew it down making a knot.

"What about Sam?" I asked.

"He's probably with Hui Aloha. Makana is right. Whenever one of those priests wants anything they call on Sam to do it."

I watched him weave and loop the netting needle. While he talked he drew the needle around and formed a knot.

"Why aren't you at the clinic?" he asked.

"No work today. The Honolulu doctors are here to inspect."

"You should be up at the crater with your girlfriend."

"She's a friend, that's all," I answered.

"At your age I was married already." Rico tucked the needle into the net. "Instead of going off with Paka, you should stay here and marry that girl."

"How do you know about that?"

"Lum Kup told me."

"What did he say?"

"He sees you and Paka go to the mountains and hide your horses in the bush."

"Who else knows?"

"No one you have to worry about." Rico leaned over for his bottle of beer.

"Did you tell Sam?"

"Why should I tell Sam? It's not going to work, you know. You'll die in the valley."

"Paka and I can make it work."

Rico took a swig of his beer. "Sure, it'll work for Paka. He's only interested in himself."

"That's not true."

"He's using you, boy. Paka knows he's dying. If he stays here Dutton will put him in the hospital by Christmas, he knows that. So he can die here or he can escape with a fool like you to be his *kōkua.*"

He pointed his beer bottle at me. "You'll end up taking care of him until he dies. And then you'll be too weak from living like an animal and you'll die of lung fever with the first rain." He took another swig.

"You're talking out of your head."

"What? You think you and Paka going to go off and live forever?" He tossed the beer bottle toward the ocean.

"You're drunk, old man."

"Better to stay here. Die with friends."

"I got to go," I said, and headed back to the road.

"Loa," he called. I stood still, but I didn't turn back. "You'll die up there."

He's an old fool. A drunken, old man.

"You are going to die, all alone."

"I'm not going to die!" I shouted.

I am not going to die! The rest of them will die, but somehow I will survive. I wasn't going to die.

I rode off toward the girls' home to look for Kamalani. I had to fight Rico's words echoing in my head.

"I'm not going to die." I said it out loud. "I am *not* going to die."

I hated the *lēpela* and I waged my war against it. At night, in bed, I felt it eating my body—like a centipede crawling over me, and I killed it, crushing it, making my body clean.

Like A`ai, I had nightmares that death's feral pig came to my bed and I stabbed it over and over.

There was no sign of Kamalani, not at the Bishop Home, nor the clinic. I even tried out near the guava orchard. So I headed out to the beach by myself. I sat in a small cove tucked under a ledge of lava. The sand was dry and the smell of seaweed was strong. A curtain of morning glory hid me, and through the vines I watched as each wave pushed a blanket of seaweed farther up the sand.

From somewhere in the cove I heard a cricket. It was hiding, like me, in a sanctuary of stone.

Oh, Jehovah, make the fear go away.

* * *

The next week Dutton sent me out to inventory the livestock and horses. On June 9, 1898, there were 235 horses, 288 mares, 74 colts,

18 steer, 25 heifers, 10 oxen, 1 bull, and 25 jackasses.

The following week I had to count the trees—45 Japanese plum, 50 eucalyptus, 50 alligator pear, 18 papaya, and 4 pomegranate.

I liked doing inventories. I got to be alone and I could ride wherever I wanted. I could sleep in an open pasture and eat my lunch whenever I wanted. I laid on the grass and watched the clouds float over the mountains and listened to the doves coo.

I had fallen asleep in the sun when I was awakened by a coolness on my face. It was Paka's shadow. He was eating what was left of my lunch.

"I heard next week's shipment is full of tools—crowbars, shovels, and pipes," he said.

I leaned up on my elbow. "Oh, please, Paka. Why don't you eat some of my lunch?"

He got out a thanks between shoving the rest of my food in his mouth. "We could use a crowbar and some resin," he said. "Liniment and zinc oxide would be good, too."

I grabbed my lunch pail. "I already took twelve pounds of resin, ten pounds of zinc oxide, and rubber plaster too—we're set for bandaging," I said.

"Good." He took a swig of my water. "In two weeks we'll be gone."

"Two weeks," I repeated.

I began measuring time not by day or week, but by how long it was until our escape. It was June 26, four days away, and I still wasn't sure what I would tell Paka.

During breakfast I wanted to tell Paka I was beginning to have doubts—that I wasn't sure it was worth trying. But I didn't.

Tonight, I thought, I'll tell him after dinner.

At work Brother Dutton greeted me with an oversized box wrapped in brown paper and tied with twine. It was a package from my parents that had finally arrived. "It's for my birthday," I said.

"How old are you, William?"

"Sixteen."

"Loa, take the day off, I can manage."

I headed back to the dormitory. There was a buggy parked in front. Two new boys had arrived. Paka introduced me to Ioane Nahuna`e. He was about eighteen and already disfigured by the disease. The other boy was about eight years old. His name was Hiapo, meaning first-born child.

Hiapo was standing at the front door. He stood riveted to the floor, his knickers dripping water on the painted planks. He was clutching his leather suitcase, quietly surveying the room.

"Your bed is over here." Paka slung Hiapo's luggage on his mattress.

The boy followed. His leather shoes squeaked water as he walked. His eyes were as black and round as polished *kukui* nuts and his skin was as brown as its bark. His lips were full and his jaw square, and if it were not for the darkness of his skin we could have passed for brothers.

Both Ioane and Hiapo started unpacking. Paka wrung out Ioane's clothes.

I laid my package on my bed and opened it, the whole time listening for Hiapo—waiting for him to cry or ask me questions, or if he would just lie down and go to sleep.

My parents sent me sugared pineapple, mango peel, beef jerky, and two shirts in the new style of plaid. There was also a letter from them.

"Hiapo, do you like sweet pineapple?"

He shook his head no.

I walked over to his bed and helped him unpack.

"How about beef jerky? My mother makes good beef jerky." I folded his shirts and put them in a pile.

"No," he said.

"My name is Loa. I'm from Honolulu," I said, as I put the shirts in his middle drawer.

"I'm from Kula," he said.

"I've never been to Maui," I said.

I put his trousers in the bottom drawer. "At home my shirts are in the bottom drawer," he said.

So we shifted his clothes around like they were at home and

shoved his luggage under his bed.

"I have a horse. You want to go for a ride?"

Finally, I got a smile.

"Change your clothes and I'll wait for you on the verandah."

Paka and Ioane were already off on a tour of the compound. They were smacking each other on the back and ducking each other's false jabs.

Before Hiapo and I rode to the pasture I took him by Brother André's office to borrow two red kites. The two of us rode Niele past the guava orchards. We flew our kites high in the wind, until they were two small dots against the green mountains.

I knew it had been a long day for Hiapo, and I was surprised he was still awake, but on the way home he fell asleep leaning against me. When I tucked him into bed that night he perked up enough to tell me stories about his three-year-old sister Pualani, his baby brother Manu, and his cousin, Solomon. Solomon was older and bigger than Hiapo, and he lived next door to Hiapo. They would have *liliko'i* fights and bombard each other with rotten fruit. Sometimes Hiapo would hide in the tree house they had built last summer.

Hiapo told me about fishing with his father and the time he caught his first *pāpio*. He told me his father would read him stories at night and together they would pray. And so together he and I said evening prayers, and we asked God to bless his family and keep them all well.

"Get some rest," I said, "and maybe tomorrow we can go fishing." I heard myself sounding like my own father.

As I got up, Hiapo reached for my hand. "Loa, am I going to die?" he asked.

I looked down at his face.

"Some day. But not for a long time." I kissed his forehead.

"Loa," Hiapo asked, "would you *lomi* my stomach?" He lay on his back with his hands at his side and I massaged his belly.

Hiapo's disease was already advanced. The *lēpela* had left his face clean but his skin color was ashen. His voice already rattled and drool seeped from his mouth. I propped two pillows under his shoulders to ease his breathing.

"Is this better?" I asked.

"Thanks." His breath had the stench of a gas formed from decay.

* * *

I was sitting on the verandah writing a letter to my parents when Paka came back.

"You already writing in your journal?" he asked.

"It's a letter home," I answered.

Paka took a grass stalk out of his mouth. "You're not telling them about Pelekunu, are you?"

"No."

"Good," he said. "I don't want any bounty hunters knowing where we are."

"Don't worry, Paka. No one will know where we are."

"It looks like Mahina will bless us." Paka pointed to the white wafer moon. It was almost full. "We go in four days," he said.

"Four days," I repeated.

Chapter 8

The Decision

Four more days.

I went to the clinic early that day. It was supposed to be my last day before my escape. Kamalani was sitting in the back yard shelling peas at the picnic table. I sat and took some peas out of the bowl and popped the pods, tossing the plump, round peas into the bowl.

"Do you ever think about getting out of this place?" I asked her, keeping my eyes down on the splintered table.

"That's all I thought about when I first got here."

"Do you still think about it?"

"Sometimes." She scooped up husks and put them in the scrap bucket.

"When?" I asked.

"When the sisters tell me what to do, and what to wear and who to talk to."

Kamalani covered her hair with her apron to mimic the sisters' veils. She scrunched up her face and wagged her finger as she spoke. "A lady doesn't sit on the ground, a lady doesn't run, a lady swims clothed . . . and drowns!"

She laughed as she pulled down her apron. She ran her fingers through her hair and lifted it, and as she did the sun caught its color and the breeze carried it high. "I'd give anything to be standing under a waterfall." She stretched out her arms. "I would squeeze shampoo ginger on my hair and rub it with oil."

She let her hair fall. "Actually, I would settle for a swim at the crater." She looked at me. "Have you ever been there?"

"Paka and I ride past there every day."

"I wish I could go. . . . Maybe sometime you could take me."

"Sure."

"We could go Sunday." Kamalani smiled.

"Maybe." I wanted to tell her I wouldn't be there on Sunday, I wanted to tell her all about the escape. I even wanted to ask her to come. "I heard some patients escaped to Pelekunu two years ago," I said.

"`Ōpūnui told me about them." She kept shelling the peas.

"Did you ever think about going there?"

"When `Ōpūnui told me, I laid awake at night and plotted the whole escape. I made a list of everything I would need and who I could trust to help me."

The ringlets of her hair glowed red in the sun. "Whenever the nuns told me 'what a lady would do,' I thought about being in the valley and never having to listen to them again."

"What happened?"

"I knew I'd never go." She looked up at me. "But when I get angry, sometimes, I still think about it," she said. "Why all the questions? Are you thinking about escaping?"

I didn't answer.

"I won't tell." She put her hand over mine and smiled.

"I think about it a lot," I said. "But mostly I think about if I could do it . . . if I could make it on my own, just me—not depending on anyone else." I clasped her hand. It was the first time I had touched her.

"When I really think about living in the valley," she said, "I think everything would be the same as here . . . but worse."

I shook my head. I didn't understand.

"At least here we do something. We see patients . . . "

"Loa! Loa! Hurry!" Sister Augustine yelled from the back door of the doctor's office. "Hurry! `Ōpūnui needs help!"

`Ōpūnui had a man pinned against the wall of the doctor's office, the man's forearms locked over his head. The man was kicking and squirming and trying to butt `Ōpūnui with his head. `Ōpūnui was tucked low, burying his head in the man's chest.

The office smelled of ammonia, alcohol, and liniments—of everything trickling from bottles smashed on the floor. My eyes teared.

"Loa, get over here!" `Ōpūnui yelled.

The man kicked wildly.

"Move in!" `Ōpūnui forced me to move closer. He was straining to hold the man's arms back. The man was bearded and stinking of cigars and rum.

I squatted down on the floor and tackled his legs at the knees. *"Lā`au ho`ōla `ole. Lā`au ho`ōla `ole."* The man started crying. Medicine that doesn't cure. Medicine that does nothing for life.

"Get some bandages, Sister," `Ōpūnui ordered.

"Lā`au ho`ōla `ole."

"Tie his wrists, Sister." `Ōpūnui turned the man, and Sister Augustine tied his hands behind his back with strips of bandage.

The man didn't struggle, he had given up. His name was Akiona Palapala. His wife had died from *lēpela* that morning. She was twenty-two.

`Ōpūnui guided the man through the broken glass on the floor out to Sheriff Akana who had come to take him away. `Ōpūnui and I swept up the slivers of glass bottles and the medicine powders while Kamalani collected the doctor's books.

Sister Augustine went out to the clinic to help calm the patients.

Much of the clinic's medicine was ruined. But it really didn't matter. Most of the patients took the *haole* doctor's medicine at the clinic. Then they took the bottles home, poured out the medicine, and after they simmered their plant remedies, they used the bottles to store it.

Some patients smoked opium to relieve the pain, some had the *kahuna* chant over them. Some would rub themselves with Japanese oil, European liniment, or poultice of *noni*. They used wild ginger, turmeric, beeswax, and lard, papaya juice and tobacco, dog manure and molasses, scurrying from one cure to another until they collapsed in despair.

They rubbed their hands with ash water and salt, slept with splints tied to their hands, all to keep their fingers from curling.

"It's not as bad as it used to be," `Ōpūnui would say when he told me stories about when the doctors wouldn't go near patients and left their medicine on cottage gate posts and when ministers would preach from empty balconies, isolated from their congregation seated below. "It's getting better," he would say.

Sister Augustine swung open the door. "The doctor needs help with a tracheostomy," she said.

"Come, Loa," he said.

I put on a white coat and gloves and watched as the doctor began to cut. The patient, a woman about twenty, was lying on a table with her neck raised by a pillow. She had sniffed ether and seemed half asleep.

The doctor felt her neck and measured it with his fingers, just like Paka had showed me at the beach.

`Ōpūnui handed the doctor a scalpel. He made a horizontal cut, just where Paka had done with his thumb. He cut fast and there was no blood. I had expected a spurt of blood to pump from her neck, but the cut was bloodless.

The doctor leaned over. He probed her neck with his fat white fingers while `Ōpūnui soaked up the little bleeding there was with a rubber ball suction.

"Get her an injection." The doctor ordered `Ōpūnui to inject a drug into her exposed muscles while he pulled a ring of her trachea from her neck and twisted in a small tube.

"Head up," the doctor ordered. "Now."

I flexed the patient's head up so the doctor could sew stitches on the top and bottom of the tube.

"Head down."

I lowered her head on the bed and moved the pillow as ordered.

The doctor coaxed the tube into place with his pinkie. "Good," he said to himself. And he peeled off his gloves and walked away, leaving `Ōpūnui to finish tending the patient.

I brought `Ōpūnui a clean basin of water, gauze, and towels.

As he cleaned the wound he reviewed the procedure. "Did you notice how he cut?" `Ōpūnui asked. "Not deep. If you cut too deep you can damage the voice box or cut right through the trachea."

I wiped the woman's face and hair while `Ōpūnui bandaged her neck.

"The angle of the scalpel is important. Did you see that?" He talked with rote precision. "You must make sure the incision is dry and give the patient something to keep from coughing. Use rum if you have to."

`Ōpūnui told me what to do if there was bad scarring from the cut, or if an infection developed or if the tube collapsed. I memorized his every word. And for the rest of the day while I sat treating patients with ringworm and ulcerated feet, I could only think about my escape.

* * *

It was the night of the escape. Mahina did bless us. The moon was a glowing white ball with a bluish red halo. The sky was clear and the heavens were filled with stars.

Paka was crouched down in the shadow of the stable. "Over here," he whispered.

I sat with my back against the stable wall.

"Where's your stuff?" he asked.

I don't remember how I told him I wasn't going. I remember Paka pinning me against the wall and pummeling my gut. I couldn't breathe. I doubled over on the ground and sucked in for air.

"I knew it," Paka yelled. "I knew I couldn't count on you." Paka was standing over me. "Prince Loa, Prince of the Clinic." He paced back and forth. "Why the hell did I ever think I could trust you?"

He lifted me off the ground and threw me against the wall. "I knew it. I knew you'd never come." He started crying.

Pain shot from my back up my neck. He bashed me against the wall again. My neck snapped, my head bounced off the wall. A flash of white light blinded me and I felt myself fall. Paka's face was a blur and I could hardly hear him. It was like he was in another world.

I shook my head, trying to clear my vision.

"Dutton's little boy," he said mockingly.

I felt the wetness in my mouth—salty blood, smooth, sweet-tasting blood.

"When did you change your mind?" He leaned over me. "When?" he yelled.

I tried to cover my ears, but he grabbed them and spread my arms over my head and he yelled even louder, "When?"

I didn't answer.

He tossed me to the ground. "Coward."

"I'm not a coward," I said.

"Worthless, rich-boy coward." He spat at the ground near me.

I staggered to my feet. "I'm not a coward."

"Too much *panipani* with that rich whore at the clinic!" he said.

I lunged at him and got in an uppercut to his ribs. I saw his face. He stared at me, then dove at me with his head. I sidestepped him, and he had to stagger to catch his balance.

"Paka, let me explain," I said. "Just listen to me."

"Why did I ever waste my time with you?"

"Listen!" I said.

"I should never have trusted you. You and your royal blood. Rot in hell!"

I swung at his face, but he dodged it and caught me square on the jaw. My jawbone banged against its socket. The pain burned heat that shot down my legs. My knees buckled and I felt nauseous. I started going down.

I tried to stay up. I stumbled toward Paka and landed a punch that left us both on the ground. Lying next to him, I heard the gurgle of his breathing.

I remember staring up at the moon and thinking how sweet the smell of the new grass was, how salty the sea air. It was awhile before I leaned up on my elbow. "Are you all right?" I asked Paka.

"Do you think you could hurt me?" Paka turned his head and grinned. There was a red line of blood between his teeth.

I hurt everywhere. I felt the surge of blood throb in my hands, my ribs stung, my face was pounding. I sucked on my lips and swallowed blood.

"Loa," Paka whispered.

My shoulders jerked out of control and my hands started to tremble.

Paka rolled over and leaned on his elbow. "Loa, you coming with me?"

I shook my head no.

"All right," he said.

After a while he made it to his feet. He held his hand out for me and I took it. As I got up, he jerked me close to him and threw a left hook to my head. My eye flooded with blood. I fell back and landed against the lava wall. I couldn't see. I felt myself sliding down the wall. My shirt was caught on the rocks and my back was scraping against the stones as my feet slid down in the dirt.

I felt a kick to my ribs. I could hear Paka pacing. "Why did I waste my time with you?" he said.

"That's where I'll be." He was crying. "Open your eyes! Open them!" Paka was pointing toward Pelekunu. "That's where I'll be, while you're here dying in this stinking place. I'll be free."

"I don't need you," he said. "I don't need anyone." Paka grabbed my shirt. "Get up. Get up and look at me." The moonlight shadowed the tumors on his face.

I gripped the edge of the wall and got to my feet.

Paka jabbed at his chest as he paced. "Look at me! I'm Paka

Ki`ilehua, and I don't need anyone!"

"Paka, stay," I said. "I'll take care of you. Just stay. You don't have a chance if you go by yourself."

"Take care of me! I don't need you, *haole* boy."

"Paka, stay. I promise I'll take care of you. I promise. . . . I'll make sure you never go to the hospital. . . . I'll work it out with `Ōpūnui."

"I know your promises, boy," he said. "You going to promise me again now? Liar!"

From the very beginning, I always knew I was never going to escape. I was playing a game—pretending I was like Paka. But once I started I couldn't tell him that I was the one who was the great liar. Paka was the con man, the thief who stole from the dead, and I was the trusted one, the smart one. But I was the real fraud.

He started up to the trail.

"Paka, you'll die if you go alone."

"I thought you were my friend," he said, and walked away.

I laid down and let my body drift to sleep. It was just before dawn when I came to. With each breath my temples pounded, and my ribs sliced a razor in my chest. I looked around for Paka, but he was gone.

I looked over at the bay shimmering in the moonlight. Mōkapu Island was lit, like a sign of welcoming hope at the mouth of the Pelekunu Valley. "God watch over you, Paka," I whispered.

I rolled on my side and leaned on my elbow. My mouth was dry and my lips were crusted. My stomach jerked and I heaved a pool of blood. I tried to stand but my balance failed. My arms dipped and rose like a tightrope walker. I lumbered along, sometimes crawling like an animal, and somehow I made it back to my bed before dawn.

I walked past Paka's bed—his plumped pillows were masquerading as his body curled under the blanket. I knew it would only be a matter of hours before the brothers would discover that he was gone.

Why couldn't you see just a little good here, Paka? I thought. I was angry at myself for leaving him and angry at him for leaving me behind.

Jehovah, forgive me.

It was Brother André who woke me. I opened my eyes to a blur of a shadow of a bushy gray beard and a black robe. As my eyes began to focus, I saw his clear blue eyes.

"My God, what happened to you?" he said.

He traced the cuts over my eye. I winced.

"Did Paka do this?" he asked. I didn't answer.

He pulled a handkerchief from his sleeve and dipped it in the ceramic basin on my table. "We have to get you cleaned up before Brother Dutton sees you." He dabbed my cheeks and wiped my forehead. "Dutton wants to know where Paka and Ioane have gone."

"Ioane?" I asked.

"Yes, the new boy from Ni`ihau."

Brother André ran the cool cloth through my hair and down my neck.

How could Paka have taken Ioane? I thought. After all his talk about not needing anyone. After all these months of us planning together, then, just like that, he took Ioane.

"Loa, you need some tincture on these cuts."

I glanced over to see Ioane's bedsheets pulled down and a row of pillows shaped in the form of a body.

Brother André's handkerchief felt like gravel scraping my face. "Sheriff Akana is in Dutton's office," he said.

Sheriff Akana had been a bounty hunter for the Board of Health before he got the *lēpela*. Even in Kalaupapa, he still hunted us down.

When I arrived at Dutton's office there were five horses tied to the post next to the flagpole. Niele was there, ready to ride. Tracking dogs slurped water from tin plates, and the deputies leaned back on their chairs with their feet on the verandah rail. As I walked past them I could smell the stink of last night's beer.

Dutton was sitting at his desk. He was holding down a rolled map as Sheriff Akana traced the map with his finger. Sheriff Akana was a mustached man, a *hapa*-Hawaiian. He was leaning over the desk. His jacket was unbuttoned and I could see the billy club tied to his belt. I remember the sound of the sheriff rapping his fingers on the map and the ticking of the clock on the wall.

"Good morning, Brother," I said.

"It is a difficult morning," Dutton said. He slid his glasses up the bridge of his nose as he looked up. "Sheriff Akana is here to question you about Paka and Ioane's disappearance."

The sheriff smoothed out his mustache. "I will come to the point, boy," the sheriff said. "We know you assisted Paka in his escape. We suspect you had planned to escape yourself. Obviously from your condition you and Paka came to blows. We need to know where Paka and Ioane are and if they are armed."

I said nothing. In the distance I could hear the brothers singing their morning prayers.

"It is for their own good," Dutton said.

"Listen, boy," the sheriff said. "You can be found guilty of aiding a settlement patient in an escape." He too reeked of liquor.

"And if I don't what will happen?" I asked.

"You could be expelled from the compound," Dutton said. "You would be forced to live on your own."

I looked around Dutton's office—there was a shipment of boxes to be sent back to the widows, parents, and children of the settlement dead.

"I can live on my own," I said.

"We know you have friends at the settlement," the sheriff said. "I've sent for Sam to be questioned. The consequences will be even more severe for him if he knew about this escape."

"Sam didn't know anything ," I said.

"So you were part of this escape." The sheriff sat up.

"Yes." I didn't want Sam to get in trouble. My thoughts bounced back and forth. I always knew I was never going to go with Paka, so there was no reason to say anything to Sam. But maybe I should have told him what I had planned. Maybe Sam could have helped me tell Paka. Most of all I didn't want Sam to think I was lying to him.

When Sam came in the office I wanted to explain everything

to him, but I couldn't. I couldn't say anything, not in front of Dutton and the sheriff. Besides, what could I say? I had lied to Paka, I had led him on.

Sam picked up my hands. My fingers were probably broken.

"Did Paka do this to you?"

"We fought," I said.

"About what?"

"I decided not to go," I said. I was ashamed. I wanted Sam to hold me, and forgive me.

"What about the other boy, Ioane?" Sam asked.

"I didn't know he was going," I said.

"We need information, *now,*" the sheriff said to Sam.

Sam looked directly at the sheriff and spoke slowly as if he had some command over him. "Give the boy time, Akana."

"There's no time," he answered. "If we don't find them by nightfall, they'll be lost."

Sam turned to Dutton. "Brother, may I speak to Loa alone?"

The sheriff and Dutton exchanged glances. The sheriff nodded yes. The sheriff went out to his men, and Dutton walked toward the back room.

Sam lifted my chin and examined my face in the morning's light. "Your face needs to be tended to," Sam said.

"Brother André is taking care of me," I answered.

"Rico told me you've had this escape planned for months," Sam said. "You never mentioned it to me, Loa."

"I'm sorry," I said. I knew it would take too long to explain.

"I treated you like my own son," he said.

I never felt such shame. "I was never going to go." That was the truth. But it didn't matter trying to explain to Sam.

"Paka and the other boy will die out there," Sam said.

"I think they can make it," I said. "They're going over the *pali* to Pelekunu Valley."

"And what will they do there? Die from lung fever."

"Paka is clever."

"Loa," he said, "Paka is not worth the trouble you'll get from the sheriff."

"I can't be a *pekapeka*." I can't be a stool pigeon. I couldn't betray Paka anymore.

"You'll be saving Paka's life." Sam put his hand on my shoulder. "Paka's dying. You're his only chance."

"All right. I'll tell them," I said. Not the truth, but a good lie. I thought of every trail I knew and figured out which one would lead the posse the farthest away from Paka.

I told the sheriff I would take him to the cave. The posse mounted their horses and I led them toward Kalaupapa, past the clinic up to the mountainside. When we got to the promontory where the Father Damien monument was, we dismounted.

We were on the opposite side of the peninsula, three miles from where Paka and Ioane had escaped.

"I stored our supplies over there, in Mad Nehoa's cabin. Nehoa would help us, he'd watch out for us when we would go up the trail to our cave."

Rico had told me that Nehoa was a boot maker on the Parker Ranch before he got the *lēpela*. He got here in November of '94 and by Christmas he was crazy. Sister Augustine said it was a symptom of *lēpela*, but Rico said he missed his family so much he went mad.

It was a lie that Nehoa had helped us, but I knew the sheriff couldn't question him—he had stopped talking years ago—now all he did was laugh.

As we rode to the clearing, I told the sheriff about the escape plan. I told him Paka and I were going to climb the trail to topside Moloka`i, near Kaunakakai, where Paka's relatives were going to meet us. They were supposed take us to a hideout in Hālawa Valley where we would be safe until they could smuggle us to Kaua`i. Once we got there, we would live at Nā Pali with more of Paka's family.

We crossed the bridge and dismounted at the clearing on the other side. The sun was shining and there was a buzz of bees and cooing of doves.

A deputy pulled out Paka's shirt and held it out for the dogs to sniff. The dogs nudged the ground around the palmettos and started up the trail, wagging their tails and nipping at each other's ears.

About a quarter mile up the trail, the dogs started yelping. They circled a sack and dug into it with their paws.

We had stumbled onto a campsite—tin pans, warm fire ashes, and a burlap sack that the dogs were attacking. The sheriff opened the sack to find a side of salted beef. The dogs strained at the leash toward the meat, but the deputies yanked them off the meat and gave them Paka's scent again. The dogs pawed at tree roots as they headed farther up the trail.

We were halfway up the cliff when we took a break. The sheriff came up to me. He had no eyebrows and the sweat ran into the creases of his eyelids. "Is this the trail, boy?" he asked.

"Yes, sir, it is," I answered.

"The boy's sending us on a wild goose chase," one of the deputies said.

"I'm not, sir," I said. "Sometimes, after a rain, we took a different trail topside. It starts up there." I pointed ahead, to nowhere in particular. "It meets up just around the bend."

"Are you lying to me, boy?" The sheriff said.

"No, sir," I said. "Look." I pointed to a rock ledge that protruded over an ohia tree. "The trail meets there, right before the ledge."

I hoped that my memory was right.

At the first bend, the trail narrowed to a muddied rut. The sheriff ordered one of the deputies to stay behind with the horses. Now there were only three of them with me. The odds were getting better, I thought. Maybe I could grab the sheriff's rifle or get away. But then what would I do?

We shuffled, single file, over decayed leaves and fallen logs. I wiped the sweat off my face and swatted the attacking mosquitoes. The deputies kept their jackets on. Under their arms and down the middle of their backs was a thick wet line of sweat.

"Loa, how much farther?" The sheriff asked.

"Not far," I said.

We moved on, through clouds of swarming gnats. At the second bend we met the trail—just where I had told the sheriff it was, but it was overgrown and there was no evidence of anyone having been there.

The dogs kept their snouts to the ground, sniffing the moss-covered stones while the sheriff slowly circled behind them. He was pounding his billy club in his hand in a slow rhythm to match his pace.

"You lied to me, boy," the sheriff said, still pounding his club as he walked toward me.

"No, sir."

"You sent us on a false lead."

"No, sir."

"Then where's the trail?" he leaned into my face and whispered.

"There is no trail," I said. "We built a raft." I was desperate to say anything. "We were going to . . . "

He slammed the club across my stomach and all of the pain of the night before flashed through my body.

"There's no raft," he said.

I doubled over, hugging my belly.

"You're a liar, boy." He cracked the club on my back. I just laid there wishing to die. I had no reason to live.

"Pick him up," the sheriff ordered his deputies.

When we got back to Kalawao the sheriff told Dutton that I had lied. He recounted every detail but never mentioned beating me with his club.

Dutton slumped over his desk. "William, you are one of my great disappointments." His voice was as cold as a lawyer's.

I should have felt shame, but I didn't. All I could think of was Paka and helping him make it a little bit farther.

"William, you will be confined to your dormitory. You will have no visitors," Dutton said. "You will no longer do work for me. I will pack up any personal items you have in the office. Pick them up in the morning and make sure nothing of yours is left behind."

"I'm sorry," I said. It just came out of my mouth.

"It is unfortunate," Dutton said. "I thought you were different."

In his own way Dutton was a fair man. He was being just, in his military fashion. It wasn't until years later that I realized how deeply I had hurt him.

I went back to the dormitory and laid on my bed. Pain pulsed through every bulging bruise. There was no part of me that didn't hurt.

I laid there watching a spider crawl up the mosquito netting over my bed, and I let sleep overtake me.

Chapter 9

The Tree House

I woke the next morning to see Hiapo standing at my bed, holding back the mosquito netting. His eyes were sparkling and his smile was broad. I remember thinking that he must have been born smiling.

"*Aloha kakahiaka.*" I wished him a good morning.

He grinned.

"Is there something I can do for you?" I asked.

He cupped his hands like binoculars and focused in on my face.

My belly ached, my hands, my chest, my head—every part of me hurt. Even talking made me feel nauseous.

"You look like a dead chicken," Hiapo said.

"I feel like a dead chicken," I said.

"Brother André wants to see you," Hiapo said. "He's in the

kitchen."

I leaned on my elbow and let my feet drop to the floor. I dragged myself out of bed and got dressed. I moved slowly, with as little movement as possible. I followed Hiapo to the kitchen, plodding along on my wobbling legs.

Hiapo knocked on the kitchen screen door seven times—two short raps, three long, and two short again. The smell of frying sausage and biscuits made me gag.

Brother Luis swung open the door and wiped his hands on a towel tied to the front of his apron. "Oh my saints, Inspector, I'm so glad you've come!" he said, as he leaned down to Hiapo. "My copper bowl is missing. It was a gift from Marie Antoinette to my great-great grandfather," he said.

Heat poured from the many ovens. Boys in pleated white caps scurried from bin to bin, while other boys mixed dough in large vats.

"What kind of villain would steal my copper bowl?" Brother Luis threw up his hands.

Hiapo giggled and put his finger to his mouth. "Sh, don't tell." He turned to me.

"That bowl is worth a fortune to me, *monsieur,* no matter what the ransom." The brother wiped gleaming rivulets of sweat from his beard.

"Is it worth some biscuits?" Hiapo giggled.

"Oh yes, a dozen biscuits, at least." Brother Luis crossed his chest with his arms and threw back his head with drama.

"Is it worth a pie?" Hiapo asked.

Brother Luis put his hands on his hips and made a scowl. "No, not a pie."

"Is it worth some jam?" Hiapo grinned.

"Yes," the brother said, "fresh-made guava jam—if you can get me two bushels."

Hiapo pointed at Brother André who was standing next to the kneading counter. Over his head, dangling from a wooden rod, were metal ladles, wooden oven paddles, blackened woks, and a bright copper bowl.

"There's your bowl," Hiapo said.

"Oh, thank you, *monsieur,* thank you." Brother Luis hugged Hiapo. "I promise you the best guava jam you have ever tasted."

As Brother Luis and Hiapo continued their negotiations, Brother André pulled me aside. "I have discussed your confinement with Brother Dutton," he said. "He will permit you to leave your dormitory, but you are still confined to the compound. Each time you leave you must ask for written permission and sign out in a log at the Administration Building. You will sign in with a witness when you return. You must record who you are with and where you will be."

"May I have visitors?" I asked.

"No," he said. "No visitors."

"May I return to the clinic at the end of the month?" I asked.

"That will be up to Sister Augustine," he said.

I couldn't imagine my life without the clinic. I had to go back.

"Brother Dutton has boxed up all your office belongings and left them for you at the print shop. He wants you to pick them up today."

Hiapo tugged on my shirt. "Can you take me to pick guava today?"

I looked at Brother André.

"I think it sounds like a wonderful idea, Hiapo," Brother André said.

"I don't think I could possibly ride," I said to Brother André.

"You will take the boy to the orchard after you pick up your things," Brother André said.

"Brother, please, can we go tomorrow. I'm still hurting."

"You will take the boy today," he said.

After breakfast Hiapo went straight to the stable and I went to the print shop to pick up my things. The print shop was a clapboard lean-to that was added to the back of Dutton's cottage. It was a cramped room that always smelled of turpentine and printer's ink. The closer I got the louder the snick and the clank of the type became.

There were two boys working in the shop. One was working the press, slamming his hip on the board, and the other was hanging wet pages on the line. I asked him where my things were. He handed me a parcel tied with twine. It was labeled "William Ka`ai" in the finest European calligraphy.

Dutton was always precise—in his penmanship, in his bookkeeping, in the exact moment of sunrise when he hoisted his American flag. He ate and read and prayed at the exact same time each day. He answered his mail in the order it came in and filed invoices in an orderly fashion. Even the pigeonholes in his desk were neatly arranged and all his letters were carefully tied.

Everything had a rule and everything had an order, and I was out of order. I had broken the rules and there was no place for me in his life.

I decided to go to his office, to try to speak with him. There was a lingering smell of cigars and coffee in the office, but there was no one there. Dutton drank milk, not coffee, and I never saw him smoke a cigar. The speckled coffeepot on the stove was still warm to the touch.

I walked over to my desk to see what work I would have been doing that day. I found a memo from Dutton to be sent to the superintendent. He reported that two boys had stayed out overnight and that the sheriff was in pursuit.

He wrote, "It is suspected that they have attempted an escape to Kaunakakai to be aided by family members. I am bound to discharge them as an example to the other boys, and in so doing I am attempting to save as many of the good ones that I can. Otherwise a large portion of these inmates would run out just for mischief and all the order in the home would be destroyed."

Under Dutton's signature he had underlined a final note. "I must save what I can." It was dated July 1, 1898.

So, that's what I was—an inmate needing to be saved.

I walked back to the dorm, stashed my things, and went to the stable to meet Hiapo. Niele was already saddled and had bushel baskets tied to each side of her.

Hiapo and I rode past the water tanks to the orchards beyond the crater. He shimmied up a tree. It was all I could do to stand there and hold the bushel for him as he tossed the sweet yellow balls of guava. The pain persisted.

From where I stood I could see a group of girls in the distance. They were all dressed in scarlet *mu'umu'u*. They walked two by two, carrying what I could make out to be a bushel, or bucket, between them. I wondered if they were going to the stream to wash clothes, or perhaps they, too, were on a guava hunt. I watched each girl as she walked, seeing if one of them was Kamalani.

"Loa," Hiapo called. "Here comes a big one."

"The tree over there is better," I said, and pointed to the farthest tree at the edge of the orchard. This time I climbed to the highest branch and squinted to spy on the girls. They were all too short to be Kamalani.

We filled our basket quickly, and I convinced Hiapo to ask Brother André if we could go again the next day. Brother André agreed, and the next day we took a trip to the crater, and the day after that we went halfway to Kalaupapa to pick breadfruit and berries.

The fourth day I took Hiapo for a swim at the crater lake. I took the long way around the lake and stopped several times to stare over toward Kalaupapa. It was that day that Hiapo asked me if we could stop spending so much time hunting for Kamalani!

Hiapo was clever for his age and a con artist of the first kind. He was bright, sassy, charming, and dying. His skin was already yellow, with white flaking patches that didn't perspire. His voice was hoarse and in the morning there were blood stains on his pillow.

Lēpela attacks parts of the body that are cooler than the rest— the hands, the feet, the earlobes, the nose. The cool ocean breeze that carried the perfume of jasmine fostered a dangerous bacteria breeding ground for bacteria in the throat and nose.

Hiapo and I swam at the crater lake, and the following week we went up the *pali* trail. We slid down muddy hills on giant banana leaves and almost ran into a pig. Sometimes at night we played marbles. I taught Hiapo how to juggle a ball, play cards, and cast a net. I took him fishing at the basin, and once in a while we went to the guava orchard and I looked for Kamalani.

Hiapo was always happy. I wondered if he knew he was dying. Like all of us at the settlement, he saw two or three funerals a week and we all knew eventually it would be our time, but I didn't know if he understood how soon it would be for him.

I built Hiapo a tree house. I hammered two-by-fours into a ladder and built a platform from scrap lumber in a mango tree near the shoreline. With Hiapo on my back, I would climb onto the platform where we sat cross-legged, stooped over a bag of boiled peanuts. We tossed nuts in each other's mouths and bombarded the mynah birds with our shells. We didn't hit any of our targets.

Once when we were in the tree house, Hiapo asked me, "Do you think about dying?"

At first I ignored him.

"Look!" I pointed to a hummingbird sipping nectar from the glazed sap of the mango, hoping it would distract him. The hummingbird darted away, and I reached up and plucked the fruit and twisted it open.

"Do you?" Hiapo repeated.

I didn't want to deal with talk about dying. It's unfair for an eight year old to talk about death, I thought. And it's unfair that I have to listen. I scooped out the sweet flesh of the mango with my fingers and offered it to Hiapo.

"Loa, do you think about dying?" he persisted.

He deserved an answer. "When I first got here I thought about it a lot, but not so much anymore."

Hiapo scraped out the softest pulp of the mango. "Do you think it hurts to die?" he asked.

"I don't think so."

I watched as he sucked on the hairy mango pit. He wiped his face with his scarf. "Why not?"

"Because I've stayed with people when they died," I said.

Hiapo finished the mango and went back to the nuts. Systematically he shelled them, rubbed the skins off, and made small piles that were ready to eat.

"Will you stay with me when I die?"

"What's all this talk about dying?" I reached over for one of the skinned nuts. "What about these nuts? I've never seen anyone peel the skin off nuts before."

"The skin gets stuck in my throat. It makes me choke," he said without looking up. Hiapo continued to work on the peanuts. "If you don't think it hurts to die, what do you think it's like?"

I turned away to look at the ocean. Jehovah, help me, I prayed. The ocean was dark that day, clearly marked by ribbons of jade and navy.

"I think it's like going to sleep—like when you sit in your father's lap after you've played all day, and your father rocks you, and you go to sleep with his arms wrapped around you."

"Do you think there's a heaven?" he asked matter-of-factly.

A double rainbow arched between the mountains and the ocean, at the west end of the peninsula.

"Look." A cool breeze blew a gray cloud behind the rainbow, lighting each of the colors more true. Hiapo craned his neck to see the rainbow through the tree branches.

"How could a God who makes rainbows forget to make a heaven?" I said.

"I see two." He pointed. "One for you and one for me. Do you think there are boiled peanuts in heaven?" He grinned.

"I hope so," I said, and threw a nut in the air. Hiapo tried to catch it in his mouth.

I already missed him. Sometimes when we were at the beach I would watch him stalk the sand crabs and run after shore birds, squawking at them and flapping his arms like a bird. I sifted sand with him, hunting for shark's teeth.

I thought of my friends in Honolulu and how they never had to watch anyone die. They never even had to think about death.

I wished Hiapo could live like that—be silly and happy and eat nuts with skins on them. I wanted him to live forever, but I knew that miracles didn't happen. The best I could hope for was that the days he had left would be happy.

I remember the last time we went to the beach together. Hiapo stopped to pet a stray dog at the beach. As soon as he pet him, the dog laid down in the sand with his legs apart for Hiapo to scratch his belly. "I have an idea," Hiapo said. "Let's get some *he`e*."

"Maybe tomorrow," I said. The sun was above the *pali*. It would set within an hour.

"Now," he said. "Ple-e-ease!"

"It's getting cold and you shouldn't get wet."

Hiapo clasped his hands in prayer. "I promise I won't get wet. I'll roll up my pants and I'll be very careful," he said. "Just one *he`e* to bring Brother Luis. Just for a little bit. Please."

"All right," I said, and I took him piggyback to the mouth of a cave.

Hiapo stood ankle deep in water. He rolled up his pants, just as he had promised. He leaned forward with his elbows resting on his knees, his face inches above the water. He spotted a mound of stones and poked his stick between them.

"Not there," I said. "Look for piles like these." I jabbed my stick between the stones in front of me.

Hiapo came over. "Be careful. Lift your feet," I said. Hiapo had no feeling in his feet, and he was dragging them over the jagged stones. I checked his soles for cuts. There were a few but nothing that looked deep.

"Hiapo, look." I traced the water with a branch." See these rocks. See—it's like they don't belong here." The pile was contrary to the contour of the sand.

"Like they're in the wrong place?" he asked.

"Exactly," I said. "Like they've been moved there."

"Is there one under there?" he asked.

I put my hand over his and jabbed his stick in the nooks.

"Nothing," he said. He put his hands on his hips and looked at me as if it were my fault there was no octopus. He made a few more thrusts around the pile and agitated the water. The sand swirled and clouded our vision.

"Roll the first few stones away and try deeper," I said. I stood with my back almost to the ocean, every few seconds turning to check for an incoming swell. The tide was coming in fast and Hiapo was already knee deep in water.

"I got one! I got one!" he said. A *he`e* wrapped itself around

Hiapo's stick and tried pulling it into his lair. Hiapo could hardly hold the weight of the octopus out of the water.

I took the pole and dangled his catch in front of him. It was a small *he`e*, maybe two hands long, but to him it was a grand prize.

When Hiapo poked his fingers at his captured prize, it wrapped its tentacles around his arm. "It's sucking me," he squealed.

I peeled the *he`e* off him, but not before it had left pink suction marks on his skin.

"Let me," he said, as I pushed the squid's head inside out and readied it to bite the "eye." The brain, or the "eye," protruded out for Hiapo to bite.

"Will it gush in my mouth?" he asked.

"It won't gush. It's crunchy," I said.

A wave rippled, knocking Hiapo off balance.

"Just do it," I said.

He clamped down on the *he`e* and bit. Its tentacles fell limp and it dangled from my hand.

"It's slimy," he said.

I took off my shirt and made a sack for our catch while Hiapo went back to his hunt.

"Come on, let's go," I said.

He ignored me and walked out farther.

"It's getting late, and you promised, just one catch for Brother Luis." And I waded out and took him by the hand.

Hiapo pulled back and lost his balance. He tried getting himself up and slipped and fell in the water.

"Now we have to go," I said.

He was drenched, his feet were bleeding, and he had a cut on his hands from scrambling to stand. I took his handkerchief and mine and bandaged his feet, and I piggybacked him for the mile walk home. I could feel his body shiver.

"Are you feeling all right?"

"I'm a little cold," he said. He rested his chin on my shoulder.

I kissed his arm around my neck and tasted the tang of the ocean's salt.

By time I got him back to the dormitory his lips were blue and chattering. I took off his wet clothes and rubbed him down with alcohol, put on his pajamas, and wrapped him in a blanket.

"I'm going to bring the *he`e* to Brother Luis and get some soup for you."

I asked one of the boys on the verandah to watch Hiapo until I got back.

When I returned Hiapo was congested, his breathing was labored, and his nose was clogged. I tilted his head back and examined his nostrils. They had quickly filled with bacteria and his throat had a gray coating. Hiapo was breathing through his mouth, and I knew the cool air would complicate his problem. Once it hit his throat more bacteria would grow and cut off his air supply.

"Jared, go get Brother Dutton. Tell him I need the silver nitrate and the long rods. Hurry! Now!"

He stared back at me. I scribbled a note for the boy to take to Dutton. "Here. Take this to Brother Dutton, now. Hiapo is very sick."

Hiapo reached for my hand. "Am I going to die?"

"Don't worry, as soon as Brother Dutton comes, you'll be fine." I could hear him struggle for air.

Within minutes Dutton arrived with a leather roll of instruments. Without a word the two of us worked as partners. Dutton unrolled the pouch on the dresser, unscrewed the jars, and dipped the long rods into the silver nitrate compound.

"Hiapo, I need you to be very still," I said.

Dutton lifted his head and put a pillow under his shoulders.

"I'm going to poke a hole through the infection in your nose," I said. "It's going to burn but you *must* stay still."

He nodded yes.

Dutton handed me a rod, then he cupped Hiapo's head between his hands. I leaned over and could see the tears in Hiapo's eyes. Dutton hummed a soft hymn. I held the rod between my fingers and inserted it. I had no feeling in my hands and couldn't tell if the rod was meeting with much resistance. I pumped the rod slowly.

"Stop!" Hiapo screamed. There was a smell of burning flesh.

"I've got him," Dutton assured me.

I began to enlarge the hole by rolling the long rod between my fingers and moving it slightly to the right and left. The compound sizzled as it burned his skin.

"It hurts!"

Dutton leaned over the boy. I inserted the rod again and could see the cauterized airway. The rod began to move freely and Hiapo's chest jerked, fully inflated—an airway was cleared.

Dutton released Hiapo and prepared the compound for the other nostril. Once again I had success and Hiapo calmed down.

"That was a good performance, William," Dutton said.

"Thank you, sir," I answered.

This was the first time we had spoken since Paka's escape.

"I'm sorry about the escape," I said. "I didn't mean to lie. I just wanted to be a loyal friend."

"Your loyalty was misplaced." Dutton stood up and began to collect the instruments.

"Brother," I said, "I would like to take Hiapo to the clinic." I wanted to be the one to take Hiapo to the hospital, but I still had a week left of my confinement.

With his back to me, he answered, "Go."

"I'd like to stay with him." I groped for words to help my argument, but Dutton simply said, "Stay."

"Stay as long as required and return directly from there."

I readied the horses and together we padded the buggy with blankets. I swaddled Hiapo and propped his head up with pillows. I drove to the clinic, riding as fast as I could yet trying to avoid every rut. It was beginning to get dark, and I began to pray to a God who was showing no mercy.

How is it, God, that you who make rainbows can let a child die?

I pictured Hiapo's funeral with me standing at his grave. I heard the song of the choir and Makana's tears.

I forced the thought out of my mind. I made myself think about family picnics, fishing with my friends, Sunday evenings when Papa read the Bible. I thought of the first time I saw my brother, all wrinkled and brown. I thought of the coronation parade. I thought of

Paka and Ioane at Pelekunu Valley, of Sam and Makana, of A`ai and Rico. I thought about anybody or anything but Hiapo's dying.

The moon had risen and stars began to show. The clinic's roof reflected silver and the moon cast its deep shadows. There was a light from the window that was closest to the door.

The night duty attendant and I carried Hiapo into the clinic. We put him in an iron bed with a high headboard and tall side rails. He looked so small.

There was a Chinese man in the bed next to him. He was curled up like a child. Next to him was a Hawaiian boy, maybe twelve or thirteen. There were eight beds—six of them were filled, three of them with children. The ward smelled like a freshly slaughtered deer, bleach, and brewing coffee.

The assistant returned with Sister Augustine following behind. A few strands of *haole* red hair stuck out from her white headpiece.

"What's happened, Loa?" she asked, as she began to examine Hiapo.

As I explained she unbandaged his neck and examined the surgery.

"Good job. You probably saved his life," she said.

I'm the one who got him sick, I thought.

"I'm sure he'll be fine," she said.

She worked herself around the bed toward me. She traced the scar above my eyebrow. "I heard the sheriff beat you."

"No," I said. "I had a fight."

She raised my chin and examined the bruise at my temple. Her breath smelled like stale coffee. "Quite a fight, I'd say," she remarked. "Has Paka sent any word to you?" she asked.

"No."

As we talked she bathed Hiapo.

"I'd like to come back to the clinic," I said.

"That's fine," she said.

"Brother Dutton told me it's up to you," I said.

"As soon as you can arrange it," she said.

I thought she agreed too quickly. Maybe she didn't understand. "I tried to escape, you know," I said.

"I know," she said. She sat in the chair next to Hiapo's bed and leaned the chair back on its back legs. "If I were your age, I'd try to escape myself."

"Why do you stay?" I asked.

"I can't imagine being anywhere else," she said. "It was God's will for me, and now that I'm following his will, I am happy. But I didn't understand that at first." She rested her head against the wall. "The first year I was here I wrote letters to my superior asking for a transfer. Every week I would write a different reason for leaving. I wanted to escape too. She righted her chair and reached over for Hiapo's hand.

"What happened?" I asked.

"I never sent the letters," she said. "I was too proud to leave. The sin of pride." She laughed. "I would not admit defeat. I confessed my sins and prayed many nights about it. Then I came to understand that not sending the letters was my choice to stay. I was seeing God's will."

Hiapo's hand jerked and Sister Augustine stroked his arm. "We all make our choices—in different ways," she said. "You've made your choice to stay. I can only trust you more now, not less."

"Thank you, Sister."

She leaned over and kissed Hiapo's forehead. "I need to get some sleep," she said. "I'll see you in the morning, William. Would you like the orderly to set up a cot for you?"

"The chair is fine," I said.

"If you change your mind, ask Kalā for help," she said.

"Thank you, again."

"God watch over you both."

I spent the night at Hiapo's side, waking every few minutes to check his breathing.

I smoothed his sheets on his bed and noticed a change in my hands. My fingers were puffy and there was a slight curl to them.

I took my lamp into the doctor's office and turned the mirror over. My face was beginning to lose its color and my skin had a shine. As long as I was clean, and the disease didn't show, I could still trick myself into believing I would be spared. But the *lēpela* was beginning to win.

I looked at the dying patients in their beds.

I'm too strong to die. Somehow, I will survive.

* * *

By morning Hiapo's breathing had improved, and I left with him sleeping calmly. The morning attendant took over my watch, and I returned to report to Brother Dutton about the events of the night.

I slept through most of that day and the next—without Hiapo at the dormitory there was no reason to get up. The day lost its adventure and I dreaded the empty routine. One day fell into the next, until the afternoon that the July 14 issue of the *Commercial Advertiser* reached the settlement.

The headline was one word: "Annexation!"

It reported, "On July 7, 1898, President William McKinley, surrounded by his Cabinet, signed a resolution annexing Hawai`i to the United States." With a simple declaration it became official that Hawai`i as a nation didn't exist. As a country we were dead, news that had taken a week to travel from Washington to Honolulu, and another week to get to us.

That morning the routine of the men playing cards was replaced by speculation of war. There was talk about Captain Wilcox and if he would rally his troops and if the Russians or British would come to our aid.

The men, toothless and lame, misshapen and weak, boasted about what they would do if they were in Honolulu. To a man each would have single-handedly driven the *haole* from our sacred shores.

In the middle column of the paper was a drawing of the American flag and next to it was a poem by Henry M. Whitney. It read, "And the star-spangled banner, in triumph shall wave. O'er the Isles of Hawaii. And the home of the brave." Its title was "Here to Stay!" A sketch of Dr. John S. McGrew with the caption "Father of Annexation" was below it.

The paper went on to report that on July 13 at precisely 3:30 p.m. the steamer the Pacific Mail S.S. *Coptic* signaled from offshore that the Hawaiian Islands were now part of the United States. The ship's signal flashed that American flags were to be hoisted in celebration.

Two batteries stationed at the harbor responded to the *Coptic* with a one-hundred-gun salute. The reporter wrote that "thousands" flocked to the docks in joy. "The crowds were delirious," he wrote.

But the men on the verandah questioned how many in this crowd were Hawaiian.

Some of the men blamed the *haole* for the end of our nation, many blamed Kalākaua, others said they were resigned to our fate. The men talked about the glories of the Hawaiian royalty. They praised their reigns and forgot their injustices. They had no memory of burdening taxes, plundered funds, or the abuse of our people. They remembered Hawai`i as they wanted it to be, a place that never was.

That afternoon Hiapo was released from the clinic and `Ōpūnui took him back to the dormitory.

When I tucked him into bed that night I told him stories about Hawaiian kings and queens, and I too never mentioned those things that are best forgotten.

Chapter 10

The Cart

Within a week's time Hiapo had fully recovered. He was back at the dormitory charming the brothers and demanding that I take him fishing. Life went back to its comfortable routine.

Dutton met with Sister Augustine and Brother André before allowing me to return to the clinic. I spent three afternoons a week at the clinic, and my mornings I spent with Hiapo.

I was late for work my first day back at the clinic. That was the morning Hiapo insisted on seeing the newborn foal. We headed to the stable after breakfast, but on our way Hiapo had to visit Brother Luis and Ah Nee, the tailor, and Keola, the poi maker, and Luke, the barber, and Antonio Silva, the blacksmith.

As we were leaving the stable, Hiapo climbed on my back and kicked me like he was a race jockey.

"I told you if you kicked me again, you would walk home," I said.

He let go of my shoulders and slid to the ground.

"You're heavy," I said massaging my neck.

Lum Kup called out from the bullpen, "Is that how you take him around?"

"Unless we're riding Niele," I answered.

"A cart would be better." He walked toward us.

Hiapo threw his hands in the air. "Why don't you make me a cart?"

"Because I didn't think of it," I said. "And besides, I don't know how."

Lum Kup called to Mr. Holokai. The two of them talked and told us to wait for them at Niele's stall.

Niele had been my horse for over five months and I still had no affection for her. She was an ornery nag that got me where I wanted to go, but her temperament was no better than a mule's. When I rubbed her down, she would snort. When I groomed her mane, she jerked away. I had more pleasure oiling my saddle.

That day when I dipped my rag into the oil can and watched the leather darken, I realized what feeling I had in my hands was gone. I could see the swirling pattern of the oil, but I couldn't feel the oozing of it through the cloth.

Hiapo had fallen asleep, and I swept out Niele's stall and brought in new hay. How much better it would be, I thought, if the *lēpela* would take away the sense of smell. It would making cleaning up manure easier.

My chores were all done, and I couldn't wait for Lum Kup anymore. I hoisted Hiapo on my back, and in his sleep he curled his hands around my neck and he perched his legs on my hips. He never woke, not on the way home, not even when I tucked him in bed.

I didn't want to leave Hiapo alone. For some reason that day, I was afraid. I was afraid that if I left him he would die. I thought that only I could protect him—like I had some magical power over him that could keep death away.

Hiapo is fine, I told myself. His breathing is good. He has had no fever for a week. I walked toward the door and twice I turned back to check his breathing.

I looked around the compound to scout for someone to stay with him. Most of the men in the quad were drunk from toasting their kings' past glories. There were a few older boys standing around and some younger ones jousting with stilts.

I mounted Niele and rode toward the clinic. I was past Damien's church before I doubled back. I told myself that Sister Augustine would understand that I couldn't leave Hiapo, that I couldn't go to work that day.

But instead of sitting next to Hiapo's bed I found myself standing in front of Dutton's desk.

"Yes, William." Dutton's voice was flat.

"Could you watch over Hiapo while I'm at the clinic?" I asked. "He's asleep now and needs someone to wake him for dinner."

He looked up at the ticking clock. A vine of brass ivy twined around its pendulum. "I shall visit him on the hour," he said. "Is that all?"

His words were like a brick wall.

"Yes. Thank you, Brother," I said.

Dutton nodded.

I didn't understand him. The night Hiapo was sick, I thought we had reconciled. I thought some things had passed.

Niele and I took our ritual trek to the clinic. She stopped at the Church of the Healing Water despite the fact that the minister's wife wasn't there. At the crest of the hill I watched Makana sitting with girls, surrounded with their buckets and weaving. The bougainvillea on the rock wall was in full color, spilling purple and white petals on the road.

Makana shielded her eyes as she called. "Loa!" Her *mu`umu`u* rippled as she ran. The smell of baking wafted from the cottage.

"Loa, it's so good to see you. Can you come for dinner?"

I told her I hadn't requested permission.

"What about tomorrow?" she asked.

"I can ask," I said.

"That would be better," she said. "Come early. There'll be someone else here too."

"May I bring Hiapo?" I called out.

"Of course," she said. "Tell him I'll make *kūlolo* for him."

"We'll bring some mountain apples," I called out.

"Sam has big news to tell you," she said as she walked backward to her girls.

I didn't make much of what she said. Sam probably wanted to tell me about the new recreation center, or a new shed he had built. I rode on. Ah Choy's cottage was the next landmark. Ah Choy's cottage was getting worse by the day. There were gaping holes in his roof now and his gutters were clogged with leaves.

I thought about Paka, about the night he bargained for opium, and I wondered if he was still alive.

Paka was gone, and Hiapo was fading from life. Somehow, with a small scraping of my cheek and a diagnosis scribbled by a doctor, my whole life was out of control. I had lost my family, my dreams, my friends—everything.

Niele ambled along toward the clinic. A little girl sat on the steps singing to her rag doll baby while men huddled over rain barrels playing *kōnane* checkers.

I walked into the clinic to the smell of singed hair, sweat, and blood. There was the familiar clanging of instruments tossed in metal bowls and the dragging of stools over planks. It felt comfortable.

I opened the door to the doctor's office. There were stacks of opened ledgers on the doctor's desk and a black adding machine was on the pullout shelf. I took off my jacket and hung it on the peg next to the mirror. I turned the mirror over to look at my face. "The face of the lion" was beginning. My eyebrows were thin and there was a bulge over them. My right eyelid drooped slightly.

The door opened, and I quickly flipped the mirror to the wall and put on my apron.

Sister Augustine plowed through the door. "William, good to have you back." She sat at the desk.

"It's good to be here," I said.

"How's Hiapo?" She rolled up her sleeves and sat at the doctor's desk.

"Very well, thank you."

She licked the tip of her pencil and pulled one of the ledgers closer. "I pray every morning that God will accept his soul peacefully."

She seemed to accept Hiapo's death as casually as doing her accounting. She would pray for his soul? Had she already buried him in her head?

I grabbed an armband and went out to the clinic.

"So Dutton finally allowed you back?" `Ōpūnui said.

I shrugged and tied my apron at my waist.

"Have you heard any word from Paka?" he asked.

"Nothing. Have you heard anything in town?" I asked.

"The sheriff is still looking for him. He's taken Paka's capture as his personal crusade." `Ōpūnui adjusted the armband on my sleeve. "He's even offering a ten dollar reward for information."

I put on my gloves and began measuring out our powders. "Do you think the sheriff will catch him?" I asked.

"No. But he'll try his damnedest."

`Ōpūnui took two metal trays out of the cabinet and lined up our instruments in precise rows.

"`Ōpūnui, do you know anyone who ever made it to Pelekunu?"

"When I first got here there were three clinic workers who escaped. We were all questioned for days." `Ōpūnui laid clean gauze over the instruments. "They planned that they would come back and meet some other workers on the next full moon. But no one ever came back."

Our first patient, a young pregnant woman, took her seat. I peeled the crusted bandages from her legs, trying not to strip too much of her skin away.

As we worked `Ōpūnui asked about Hiapo's condition. "How's his appetite?" he asked.

"Strong," I said, "and there's no fever. But sometimes at night he has chills."

"Is he in pain?" `Ōpūnui twisted the clean bandages around the woman's leg.

"No, no pain," I answered.

The young woman thanked us.

"And no problems with his breathing tube?" `Ōpūnui asked.

The next patient sat down. His condition was routine—scaling skin, unhealed boils.

"No, his tube is fine," I said.

"Good."

`Ōpūnui and I fell into an easy partnership. We worked together as if no time had passed since my last day. One after another the patients came and we did the best we could.

I wanted to ask `Ōpūnui about Kamalani.

"It's good to have you back, Loa." I felt a hand on my shoulder. The lightness of ginger scented the air. It was Kamalani. She had yellow ginger twined in her braid.

Before we could talk `Ōpūnui told Kamalani to get Sister Augustine. He needed her to assist with a woman patient. The woman was crying that `Ōpūnui was trying to kill her. Sister Augustine soothed the woman. She held her hand and wiped her brow, while `Ōpūnui and I worked on her sores quickly.

Sister Augustine was a good woman. She had dedicated her life to our people, but there were times, when she spoke about Hiapo's pending death, or the pending annexation, that I could only see her as a cold *haole*.

It was at the end of the day when Sister Augustine mentioned the annexation. "William, you must have heard." She was beaming. "Now you will be part of the United States. We'll be able to get better medical supplies and more American doctors. Perhaps even more sisters will be allowed to come."

"*Paha*," I said. Perhaps.

"There's even talk of a visit from the annexation commissioners." She couldn't contain her delight.

I looked at `Ōpūnui. "No, I didn't hear anything about a visit."

"There's a tour of the settlement scheduled one month after the annexation," `Ōpūnui told me.

"If they keep to the plan it will be September 11," Sister added.

"We're already planning—there will be a parade and some speeches, then a picnic at the landing."

And what is it that we Hawaiians should be celebrating? I asked myself.

On the way home I thought about the annexation. I wondered about the discussions at home. Was my mother in any danger? Would our schools be untouched? What will happen to the Queen?

The moon was almost full that night, almost as bright as the night Paka left.

When I got back to the dormitory I was surprised to see Hiapo waiting for me on the verandah.

"Why aren't you asleep?" I sat on the rocker next to him.

"Manu told me that there are spirits from the valley that are coming to get me," he said.

"Pelekunu Valley?"

"Yes," Hiapo said. "He told me they can only get you if you're asleep."

I reached over for his hand and listened to him repeat the stories about the spirits of the dead who haunted the clouds in the valley. They moaned in the night and swooped down through the settlement, coming for those of us left behind.

"A`ai told me about the spirits," I said. "But I've never heard them myself."

"Come here," I said, and he came like a shot and curled up on my lap. I told him the story of how Maui lassoed the sun, and I rocked him long after he had fallen asleep.

* * *

There was always hope in the morning, at the beginning of a sunrise. The roosters announced the dawn and the younger boys moaned about rising.

Hiapo reveled in his morning routine, his visits with Brother Luis, with the barber, the blacksmith, the tailor. They were all his willing subjects and he was their delightful king.

And on that day Lum Kup presented the king with his carriage.

It was a dilapidated rickshaw transformed into a royal horse-drawn cart.

The first design we tried was a failure. Lum Kup and Mr. Holokai nailed two-inch rails to the rickshaw, trying to make something of a yoke, but when Niele stopped, the cart slid under her. I suggested a rope tow on a one-railed axle, but the dowel I needed to steer the cart splintered my hand.

What worked in the end was one long rail nailed to the bottom of the rickshaw with a simple leather strap for me to loop my hand through. The carriage had limited maneuverability and stopping took considerable strength, but listening to Hiapo complain took even more.

"Stink!" He waved his hand in front of his face. "Niele's spraying her gas all over my head."

"Loa," Mr. Holokai said, "maybe Hiapo would be happier if he walked to Makana's house tonight."

"I don't want to walk," Hiapo said.

"Then stop complaining," I said.

"If nothing suits you, Hiapo, maybe you will have to walk," Mr. Holokai said.

Suddenly Hiapo agreed the cart was just fine.

We took a few turns around the stable before I rode the cart to Makana's. I had to hold the rail straight-armed, and when Niele took corners I had to lock my elbows hard. By the time we got to Makana's cottage my arms were aching and my wrists were laced with welts.

"E komo mai." Makana called out a welcome.

Sam took Hiapo into his arms and carried him into the house. His hands were so big they almost circled Hiapo's waist.

Makana took my arm as we walked.

"We have such good news to tell you." She was almost skipping. "I can't wait for you to know."

Chapter 11

The Announcement

The cottage smelled of fresh paint. The dining room table had piles of yellow fabric bunched around a small black sewing machine.

Makana chattered about the girls' weaving, while Sam settled in the rocking chair with Hiapo on his lap. All was normal, except for the fabric on the table.

Rico showed Hiapo a toy he had made for him. It was flat wooden bear that climbed up two ropes when you pulled on strings threaded through its paws. Rico hung the bear from a hat rail hook. He stood back, made the strings taut, pulled one string, then another, causing the bear to climb up the rope.

Makana brought out some taro pudding, and A`ai and Rico got into a fight about politics. All was normal, except for the fabric on the table. Then Makana led me and Sam into the kitchen. That's when Sam made the announcement—he and Makana were getting married.

"Congratulations," came naturally out of my mouth, but in fact, I was stunned.

"Aloha," Kamalani called out from the porch. She was carrying a basket filled with white lace and small silk flowers.

"Aloha." Makana kissed her.

"These are from Sister Rebecca." She held up the frail white blossoms. "She thought you might want to use them to trim your gown." There was an ease between them.

"Kamalani has been helping me with the preparations all month."

Sam and Kamalani hugged.

"She's an excellent seamstress." Makana fingered the lace while Kamalani pinned the flowers on the yellow cloth.

"What do you think, Sam?" Makana held the silk blossoms to the neck of her dress.

"This is when I know to leave," Sam said. "Come, Loa."

The two of us went out back. I had forgotten the scent of basil and oregano from Rico's garden—the creak of the steps, the drip from the gutter, the flapping of the fishing net hanging between trees—all unnoticed until they were missed.

As Sam and I walked to the swing he put his arm around my shoulder. It was the first time we were alone since the escape. I wanted to say something but didn't know how. I was grateful that he asked me, "Have you heard from Paka?"

"No."

He said nothing, just nodded.

"We never talked about him coming back to the settlement, or me trying to meet him. We always talked about escaping together, and we already had all the stuff we would need."

The new swing was wide and sturdy. It was made of one-by-fours bolted together and shaded by a sailcloth awning on top.

"I see," Sam said, still nodding.

"I wanted to tell you, Sam . . . but I was afraid."

"What did you think I would do?"

"It wasn't you. I was afraid because . . . if I told you . . . then I knew what you would say."

"And what would I have said? . . . Not go?"

"No, you would tell me to be honest with Paka." I looked into Sam's face. "I tricked him. I never wanted to escape." Without asking, I wanted Sam to forgive me.

"When did you tell him?"

"The night we were supposed to escape. I met him at the barn. I think he knew as soon as I got there."

"And the two of you fought."

"Yes," I said.

"And that's why you lied to the sheriff?"

"Yes."

Sam sat back on the swing and rocked.

"Paka is a smart boy," Sam said. "My guess is that he knew you wouldn't go before you did. He's not stupid—he saw you working in the clinic, he saw you with us, with Kamalani."

"I'm not sure," I said. "I think I hurt him."

"I'm sure you did," Sam said. "But Paka has taken care of himself for a long time. You don't stay at Kalawao seven years and not learn how to be a survivor, like an animal."

"I lied to him."

"Maybe when he needed someone to listen, you listened, whether you went or not. After all, he did take that new boy."

"Yes," I said. And that hurt me.

"The Burial Society is going on a boar hunt. I'll ask some men to go on the trails to look for them. Will you tell them where to go?" he asked.

"I can get them to our cave," I said.

"Good," Sam said. "The only other thing left to do is pray."

From the far corner of the house Rico appeared bouncing as he walked, pulling Hiapo's rickshaw behind him. Hiapo waved to us from his throne.

"Loa," Sam said, "I tried to get word to you about the wedding."

"I was surprised," I said.

"Was it a surprise?" Sam asked.

I shook my head "yes," not wanting to tell the truth.

"E, Sam," Mr. A`ai called out, as their motley parade headed toward us.

"Makana calls our wedding 'a celebration of hope.' "

"Does your wife know?" I asked.

"I wrote to her. She's grateful that Makana gives me comfort and she gives us her blessing."

"What about your sons?" I asked.

"They're young. They wouldn't understand."

"E, Sam, I need a carpenter." Rico took off his hat and wiped the sweat from his face with his arm.

"Loa, sometimes I forget what my sons look like. I try to remember their faces, then I try to imagine what they'll look like when they're men." Sam rested his hands on his knees, getting ready to get up.

"It's not the same as when I married my wife. We were young, and we planned children and a long life together."

"But you're going to die," I said.

"It's no secret why I'm here." He laughed.

"Then why marry?"

"Because I refuse to stop living." The skin on Sam's face shone like the handle of a well-worn ax. "The *lēpela* may take me soon, but I'm not giving up one good day to it."

"Help me, Sam," A`ai said. "This fool wants to paint the rickshaw yellow with garlands of painted flowers."

"I'll be right there." Sam waved at him.

"Loa, take a look at Rico's garden." He pointed toward the dangling forks wind chimes. "If I die tomorrow, the birds will still come and they'll still steal Rico's beans. If I'm alive or dead, they'll do the same. Life goes on, Loa."

"It's not that simple," I said.

"But it is," Sam said. "Look at the ocean."

It was a calm sea.

"And the sky."

There was a crisp blue sky with white billowing clouds.

"And the birds."

—The soaring `iwa.

"The day I die will be as beautiful as today, and the day after that will be the same."

Rico walked over to the swing. "The child wants the cart to go faster," he said to Sam.

"It's not safe to go faster," I said.

"He wants it to go faster," Sam said.

Hiapo sat, surrounded by the men, each of them with his own opinion about the cart. A`ai wanted to paint it black with gold letters with a pennant on the back. Rico wanted a brass horn. He wanted Hiapo to ride in the Corpus Christi parade. A`ai had him in the annexation protest.

"We could weave streamers through the spokes," A`ai said.

"What about your wedding, Sam?" Rico said. "Hiapo can lead the procession to the church."

"We're getting married right here, not in any church."

"Then he can welcome people at the road."

"It's up to Makana," Sam said.

"Sam, you let that woman have too many opinions." Rico lit up a cigar.

"Don't listen to him, Sam. It's the weakest men who talk the loudest," A`ai said.

"Sam," Makana called from the back door.

"Sa-a-a-m," Rico mocked. "Your woman is calling you."

As soon as Sam headed to the house, Rico pulled me aside. "Have you heard from Paka?"

"No," I said.

"He's probably dead." Rico talked with the cigar clenched in his teeth.

"Maybe not," I said.

"We'll be fishing his body out of the stream with the first good rain."

I wouldn't give in. There was no proof that Paka was dead. We each could believe our own truth, and for me until I saw his body, I knew Paka was alive.

"What about that other boy?" Rico asked.

"I don't know him."

"See, I told you. Paka would take any fool willing to go. Didn't I?"

"Yes," I said.

"The first storm, I'm telling you, we're going to find them dead."

"I've got to go inside," I said, and went into the house to avoid him.

Makana was standing on a dining room chair. Kamalani was kneeling on the floor in front of her, pinning the hem of her dress. Kamalani's mouth was full of straight pins clenched between her teeth. As Kamalani worked, Makana turned slowly. Makana talked about the wedding flowers and leis and about how much had to be done and who she could ask to help her—the porch needed painting, Sam needed to hunt a pig, she wanted squid and four bushels of `opihi.

Sam moved scraps of fabric off the rocking chair, and I cleared sheet music off the floor to find a place to sit.

Wedding talk went on through the day, and at night, as we sat on the back porch balancing our dinner plates on our laps, Makana and Kamalani were still deciding on the menu while the men turned their conversation to politics.

A`ai swirled the brandy in his glass. "We're all dead, all Hawaiians are dead from *ma`i `Amelika.*" The disease of America. He sipped his brandy and softly placed the glass on the porch rail. "There is no hope for us."

"You're drunk," Rico said. "That's what's wrong with you people. You drink too much and work too little."

Kamalani turned from her conversation with Makana and said, quite firmly, "We are hard-working people."

"And your women have too many opinions," Rico added.

The evening breeze carried the scent of gardenia, and the wind in the palms sounded like a distant rain. Hiapo was asleep in Sam's lap, oblivious of the squabble.

"She's right. The Hawaiian people work hard," A`ai said.

"They fish and they farm, but their profits are stolen by foreigners."
A`ai's hands were covered by white gloves stained with blood.

"Foreigners? It's not the foreigners who starved them—it was
your own chiefs—whoring princes and women as fat as whales."
Rico thrust his finger at A`ai. "You want to talk about greedy
bankers? Yes. Yes. Thieving Americans? Yes. But when your people
died working their farms it was to feed your eunuch kings."

Kamalani got up to clear our plates.

"Not one of them could produce a child." Rico spit phlegm into
a tin can.

"It doesn't take brains to breed. Look at you, Cabral. All you do
is make more children for your Pope."

"A`ai, you're the devil's serpent."

Makana looked over at Hiapo undisturbed by the haggling.

"I hate living with an ignorant fool," A`ai said.

"Then leave," Rico said. "Go back to Honolulu, to your brave
Opeu soldiers, sitting with sleeping dogs, reading their newspapers
while they guard the palace."

I walked Kamalani out to the swing. I could faintly hear Rico as
we walked.

"You and Dutton. You're old men with young memories."

From the swing all their voices were muffled by the surf.

"Isn't it exciting about the wedding?" Kamalani asked. She
picked prickly stickers from the hem of her *mu`umu`u* as she spoke.

"I suppose . . . if they're happy that's fine," I answered.

"Makana and I are going to twine honeysuckle vines all over
the front verandah and Rico is going to knot a canopy for their
bed." Kamalani's braid was loosely twined. "The sisters are sewing a
quilt for them, and a few girls are weaving a *lauhala* mat."

She kept picking at the green burrs. "What are you going to
do?" she asked.

"I guess I'll help with the hunt," I said.

"Is that the most enthusiastic you can be?"

"It's the best I can do right now. Yes."

"Loa, you're like a dried up old man. You never have fun."

She threw her head back and ran her fingers through her hair before she began to re-braid it.

"That's not true."

"Then what's the matter?"

"Nothing," I said.

The bells of Damien's church tolled the six o'clock hour.

"I thought we could do something for them together—something special—just from us."

"I suppose," I said.

"Loa . . ."

". . . I've got to get Hiapo back. It's late," I said.

"Loa, they're family! We need to show respect."

"Whatever you want to do, that will be fine," I said. "Just tell me and I'll do it. But I've got to go now."

Hiapo was still asleep when Sam carried him to the cart, but on the way home he woke and I had to listen to his rumblings about the stink of manure on the side of the road.

When we got back to the dormitory most of the boys were asleep, curled under their sheets, shrouded by canopies of mosquito netting.

I tucked Hiapo into his bed and quietly read him the life of Saint George the Dragon Slayer. After he fell asleep, I dragged out my trunk and rummaged through it for the envelope from the Davis Photography Shop. I pulled the netting around my bed and sat cross-legged against my pillow. I pulled out the photo of my family and I traced each face with my finger.

I tried to remember the sound of my father's voice, the smell of my mother's hair. I remembered that when Keo smiled his tongue stuck out, just a little, then I kissed the picture and set it out on my dresser.

* * *

For the next few weeks Makana's cottage was like a battle station occupied by an army of women. Women I had never seen ordered each other around. The wedding was only weeks away.

While the women planned the food and decorations, the men sat on the verandah discussing battle plans for a royalist revolution.

The men sat with their legs wide apart, straddling water casks, pounding their fists on their knees and slamming down their bottles of beer.

"Now is the time for the masses to rise," said one.

"No, it is the time for reconciliation," said another.

"We need British intervention."

"It's the Japanese who will come to our aid."

When there was a pause Mr. Holokai recited a poem he wrote mourning the stolen kingdom.

And while Sam and Makana's friends planned the wedding and revolutions, the sisters were planning for the visit of the annexation commissioners. They sewed miniature American flags and red and blue banners, and cut out white stars from old sheets. Sister Harriet calligraphed "God Bless America" on an abandoned white sign.

The settlement patients were also preparing. Many tore tattered sheets into banners and swirled crude black letters reading *"Aloha `Āina."*

The sisters taught the girls to sing "Yankee Doodle," and I taught Hiapo *"Aloha `Oe."*

After dinner one night at Makana's the seven of us ate our dessert on the porch as usual. But on that night A`ai led us in songs about the kingdom. Sam sang the low harmony, Rico played his guitar, and Kamalani joined him with her ukulele.

As the wedding drew closer the tension grew too. And more often than not, Sam and I stayed away from the house. We had already sanded the floors, painted the walls, and plumbed the back-up well. Everything that needed to be done outside was done, so we took to hiding in Kalaupapa town.

The night before the wedding we sat savoring our bread pudding and talking over what we had done to the house. The verandah railing was twined with honeysuckle and jasmine, yellow bunting skirted the door, the water barrels were draped with muslin, and the *lauhala* mats were ready to be spread.

Makana drew a deep breath and reached for Sam's hand. "You're a good man if you'll still have me after this."

"The man deserves a medal," Rico said.

"Yes, a medal—a very good idea." A`ai lifted himself, leaning on his cane. "I'll be right back, Hiapo." The rhythm of his walk, the tapping of his cane, the drag of his foot, all had become even slower.

A heavy breeze brought the smell of the night-blooming jasmine. It blew Kamalani's hair across her face. She twirled her hair in her hands and knotted it in a bun that she tucked at the back of her neck.

"Loa, how are you going to provide for a wife?" Rico asked.

Kamalani and I had become accustomed to his constant baiting.

"When the time comes, I'll provide," I said.

"We should go into business together," Rico said. "Did you see that last shipment of straw hats—terrible! Damaged goods, all busted up. The government doesn't care about us—they send us everybody else's junk."

Rico lit up a cigar. "We can start a plantation store, just like my old store. We'll call it 'Cabral's Finest.' " He flicked his match into the potted marigolds. "We can make good money—more than enough to keep a woman happy."

"Rico, I think it's you who needs a woman," Sam said. Sam had cut his hair for the wedding. His temples were almost shaved and he looked like a little boy.

Rico kept on. "We can run it better than the Board of Health store—better goods, cheaper prices. They'll be flocking to us. We can advertise 'Never a smashed hat.' "

"Dutton tries his best," I said.

"Dutton. What does he care? He's not in business. The hatmakers don't care about him. But if we had the only plantation store in the settlement we could make a fortune . . . and sell rum on the side."

"And when government ship gets delayed, you'll triple your prices!" Sam said.

"You wound me, my friend." Rico grinned. "I would simply double them."

A`ai returned with a rolled paper clenched to his chest. At first I thought he was in pain. A`ai's pain was constant. He took opium and laudanum simply to endure the day, and at times he was delirious.

With a great flourish A`ai bowed in front of Hiapo, who was curled on Kamalani's lap. "To the youngest of heroes!" He unrolled the paper and read the declaration of service given to him by Captain Wilcox. He gave it to Hiapo, then stepped back and saluted.

Hiapo smiled. "Thank you," he whispered.

Chapter 12

The Wedding

The day of the wedding had arrived.

A`ai supervised the unearthing of the pig, and Rico patted the backside of every woman who passed by him. Some of the ladies returned Rico's attention with a kiss, others slapped his hand or jabbed him in the ribs—all had a smile in their eyes.

Mrs. Kiakakone ordered Rico to shoo the cats away from the food—he willingly obliged, kicking more than a few. He rearranged bowls of sweet potatoes, tasted the guava and coconut, moved the mountain apples, and surveyed the spread of bananas, alligator pears, breadfruit, pickled ginger, fresh poi, sour poi, chili pepper, *limu*, coconut water, guava juice, tea rum, `ōkolehao, dried beef, dried fresh squid, *kukui* nutmeats with rock salt and red seaweed, split-skin pig, crusted smoked deer, whole *pāpio*, mahimahi, eels, squid, and four bushels of `opihi.

Older women wore their finest hats and men sported calico shirts. The sisters brought Makana a bouquet of roses from Mother Marianne and pots of nasturtium that they grew themselves. Sister Augustine baked molasses cookies. Lum Kup brought sandalwood sticks, and the minister's wife made *haupia.*

An old woman I had never met sat on the front verandah. Withered and deranged, she nodded at the guests as they passed, greeting them as if she were holding court. She sat with her hands gripping the head of a silver-capped cane and slightly bowed her head as each guest passed.

I went out back and stood with Sam on the back verandah. The guests were all seated on mats. Sam and I were both in borrowed black trousers, formal white shirts, black neck scarfs, and red sashes that waved in the wind like signals of distress. The music began. Sam retied his sash.

Slowly, we walked toward the minister, weaving through the mats of women whispering behind their fans. The minister stood facing the crowd. Sam and I stood to the side with our hands clasped and our necks craned to watch for the entrance of the bride.

A hushed "aah" went through the crowd as Makana appeared from the cottage. She wore a long *holokū* made of her pale yellow fabric. Her hair was knotted on her head and wreathed by a lei of ferns.

Kamalani held the trail of Makana's gown as she walked down the steps. A thick lei of *kukui* nut vines rested on Makana's shoulder. It was loosely tied above her waist. Sam's lei hung untied and blew straight in the breeze.

Sam's eyes were fixed on his bride until she stood at his side. He took her arm and his smile was sweet as a child's.

The two turned toward the minister. They faced the ocean, where there, beyond the cliff, hazy on the horizon, was O`ahu—and the lives they had both left behind.

They held each other's hands. The minister, a grand Hawaiian, wrapped a ti leaf around their hands and tugged it snug. He prayed over them and led the guests in song. From a calabash of water that was offered by Hiapo, he cupped his hands and showered the couple with the water of new life. And with a chanted blessing, he declared them married.

A cheer went up, and the party began with the couple making their way through the crowd. But before they turned to receive their friends, Sam took Makana in his arms. He held her and thanked her and told her he never felt so alive.

There were strumming guitars, ballads sung offkey, skits about lovemaking, and speculations from giggling old women. Sam toasted his bride and she danced hula for her groom.

Food was enjoyed, stories told, and gifts were placed on the lanai table. Kamalani put our book with the other presents.

I had made my last trip to the cave to get the Chinese notepaper that belonged to Ah Choy. Kamalani and I cut the sheets into neat squares and I punched holes for her to sew the sheets together. Then I shaved two pieces of *kiawe* to thin covers that Kamalani covered with *lauhala* weaving. It was a good present.

The party went on. Long into the night the *kukui* nut torches burned, the guests celebrated, and Kamalani and I slipped off to Mad Nehoa's cottage.

Rico had asked Sister Augustine if Kamalani could stay the night to help him clean. He asked Brother Dutton the same for me.

So soon after Sam and his bride left for a night in an empty cottage, I took Hiapo back to the dorm and then headed straight for Nehoa's cottage.

The cottage smelled of ginger and freshly oiled skin mixed with the pungent smell of raw leather, tanning oil, and dye.

"Loa." A square stream of moonlight fell on Kamalani's face and caught the cascade of her hair.

I had often dreamed of this night. Kamalani would be lying on the beach with her hair loose. The moonlight would fire it, glowing like lava. She would come to me like a goddess. Her lips—moist, her skin—smooth.

I let my eyes become accustomed to the dark before I stepped into the cottage.

She stood there without a sound or motion. I brushed her hair over her shoulder and lifted her chin. I kissed her eyes, her nose, her mouth. I gently guided her toward me. As we embraced she traced my spine with her hands. We were tender with each other and laid on the shoemaker's cot.

I held her in my arms and she began to cry. I leaned over her and traced her lips with my fingers. She jerked her face toward the wall.

I put my hand on her shoulder. "Kamalani."

She shrugged.

"Kamalani, please."

Slowly she turned toward me.

"Are you afraid?" I asked.

"Look at me, Loa." The moonlight cast shadows on the tumors on her face. I took her face in my hand.

"Take a good look at me." She sobbed.

I kissed her forehead.

"It's taking away my face."

I kissed her cheek.

"I want to be beautiful for you."

"You are beautiful," I said. I stroked her cheek.

"How can you look at me?"

"Because you are beautiful," I said.

"Sometimes at night I feel the *lēpela* creeping through me, like an invading demon."

I held her in my arms as she cried. "Like it's gorging itself until it has all of me and, finally, I die."

The evening breeze had chilled the air and the salt air was damp.

"I wish I was never born."

"Kamalani, wasn't it you who told me that I should love life and all that is alive?" I said.

"Those were just words," she said.

"Didn't you say that we had a purpose in life, that we help the patients." I held her closer. "Did you mean any of it?"

She snuggled her head in my chest. "I meant all of it," she said.

"But it's still not fair."

"I love you, Kamalani."

I heard my words echo. Kamalani looked up at me. I wanted her to tell me she loved me.

"Loa." She smiled. "Promise me you won't die before me."

"I'll see if I can arrange that." I smiled.

"Oh, Loa, I'm so sorry." She began crying again. "I wanted this night to be different. At night it was all I could think about."

"What did you think about?"

"I imagined that I was beautiful, and my body was clean, and my face was smooth."

"You *are* beautiful. Do I have to keep telling you?"

"Don't interrupt." She put her finger over my lips. "In my imagination, I was waiting for you under a waterfall. I oiled my hair with coconut and scented my skin with eucalyptus oil and you came to me wearing only a *malo* and you were carrying a lei of fern, berries, and vines."

"In my dreams we met at the crater lake," I said. "The water polished your skin and I could feel its coolness with my hands," I said.

"You traced my lips with red ginger," she said.

"In mine you were naked and your breasts swung freely." I combed her hair with my fingers and cradled her neck in my hands. "And your hips moved slowly with the rhythm of the tide."

"In mine we made love," she said.

And in the light of Mahina's moon, we kissed and fulfilled each other's dreams lying in Mad Nehoa's cot sheltered by a wall of half-made shoes and strips of tanned leather.

Before I fell off to sleep, I heard Kamalani's words. "I love you," she whispered.

We woke before dawn. Kamalani woke slowly. The cot patterned her cheek in a checkered web.

"I wish that we never had to leave this place," she said.

I kissed her. "We could escape," I said. "Just the two of us."

"Loa, don't even talk like that." She leaned up on her elbow, the muscles of her arms shadowed by the rising sun.

"Loa," she said, "come with me." And she got up and dragged me by the hand through the brush of tall grass to a small cave at the beach. The cave faced O`ahu. We squatted down and sat huddled inside the cave.

Kamalani cupped my hands and kissed them. "This can be our escape," she said. She brought my hands down her neck, toward the roundness of her breast.

"I love you, Loa," she said.

* * *

It was that image of her, lying in the cave, telling me she loved me, that I kept with me for the next few days. I replayed her words. I conjured up the smell of her hair and could almost feel her skin. And whenever I thought of her I wanted to be with her.

When I went back to work that day, we talked like we were casual friends, hiding the fact we were lovers.

"It was a beautiful wedding, don't you think so, Loa?" she said. "I heard lots of people saying it was better than Hokela Holt's. Even Lum Kup was talking about the food."

"I didn't get a chance to talk to him," I said.

"Truly?" She asked.

"Yes."

She lowered her voice. "Lum Kup talked to me about Paka."

"Has he been found?"

"He said the dogs followed a trail of blood up on the ridge. They found two bodies." She paused. "The bodies were so decomposed they can't be sure who they are, but they think it's Paka and Ioane."

"They buried the bodies on the ridge," she continued. "The posse should be back tomorrow."

"Doesn't `Ōpūnui know anything?"

"I don't know," she said. "He didn't say anything to me about it."

I wanted her to hold me. I wanted to rest my head in her lap and let her comfort me and absolve my guilt.

"Sometimes I think if I had gone with him we would have made it," I said.

"Or you could both be dead," she answered.

* * *

Riding home from the clinic, I thought about Paka, about what I should have said to him and what I should have done.

But my mind kept turning to Kamalani. I practiced what I would say to her the next time we met. I recited things out loud and anticipated what she would say. I remembered what we had said to each other, and of all the things I had told her, it was that I loved her that was most true.

When I got back to the dormitory I saw Brother Luis sitting next to Hiapo's bed.

"What's the matter?" I asked.

"He's had a difficult night, Loa," the Brother said.

From his tone I knew it was more than difficult.

"What time did the wedding party end?" the Brother asked.

"It's still going on," I said, looking at Hiapo. "When did he get sick? When I took him back last night he was fine," I said.

"One of the boys called me in the middle of the night. Hiapo was delirious."

Brother Luis tucked the sheets under Hiapo's mattress. "You may want to stay with him." He leaned over to kiss Hiapo's forehead.

"Loa." He put his hand on my shoulder as he left. "Death is imminent."

I watched Hiapo sleep. When he sweat I wiped his brow, when he was chilled I wrapped him in blankets. When I heard the gurgle of his breathing, I propped pillows under him, and when his head dropped to his chest, I cradled him in my arms. I sang to him and read him stories. I spoke to him, not knowing if he heard me or not. I begged him not to die and I pleaded with him to fight . . . just a little more.

More than once his eyes fluttered and, just for a moment, they opened. His eyes were blank, but when I rubbed his hand a slight smile appeared on his face.

I wanted to fight for him, to breathe life into him, but I knew all I could do was to offer him comfort. I spooned water over his lips, and I rubbed him down with alcohol.

I could hear the fluid build in his lungs, and I watched as he gasped for air. He looked like a baby bird, blindly searching for food. He arched his neck and stretched open his mouth. His body convulsed.

I held his hand.

Dear God, it's more merciful to take him.

"It's time to rest," I whispered to Hiapo. "It's time to let go."

"Rest," I told him. "Don't fight anymore."

Late that evening Father Wendolin came to administer the last rites. Brother Dutton, Brother Luis, and Brother André surrounded Hiapo's bed, and through their tears they prayed while Father Wendolin anointed Hiapo's body.

They left in a solemn procession. Each of them placed his hand on Hiapo's forehead and traced a cross with his thumb. Each kissed his forehead and said his farewell.

I kept vigil alone. I watched the rise and fall of Hiapo's every breath and waited for the next sign of movement. I was afraid to fall asleep. I thought if I slept I would abandon my guard and death would steal him away. I put my ear to his chest and listened to his heart.

In the morning Hiapo was still alive. I put my head down on the bed and fell asleep. When I awoke, Hiapo had passed on. He was at peace.

I kissed his cheek and covered his face with his sheet.

* * *

Hiapo's body was waked at Sam's cottage. Once again the men hunted for a pig and the women prepared the food. Kamalani wrapped black bunting on the cottage verandah. Makana sewed a coffin lining from her wedding dress fabric.

Sam and I moved the dining table to the center of the room and put Hiapo's coffin on it. We arranged a chair and small table next to it. There was a guest book on the table, along with a photo of Hiapo, a candle, a bowl of sand, and a Bible. A lei of ilima was draped over Hiapo's photo.

The *lēpela* is a strange disease. Right before death it almost fades away. The tumors subside, the eyes regain their brilliance, and a peace comes over the face of those almost dead. It is as if the body surrenders back to the spirit and the soul once again shines.

Once again Makana's house was filled with women scurrying around, passing out food to the mourners who clogged the house.

I sat in the chair next to the coffin. Hiapo looked like a prince. He was dressed in his woolen suit and a white shirt, with a yellow neck scarf that Sam had tied in a full Windsor knot.

He seemed like he was smiling at me, like he was telling me he was all right. It was hard to understand that he was not just asleep or only "temporarily dead." How could it be—with one breath he was alive and with the absence of the next he wasn't. He stopped being, just like that.

I watched as the mourners filed by. They touched his hand or kissed his face. Some prayed, a few cried.

Lum Kup approached the casket. He bowed, clapped his hands, and bowed again. He took a stick of incense, lit it from the candle on the table, and placed it in the bowl of sand.

A line of brothers followed. Brother Luis was first. He tucked a small wooden cross in Hiapo's arms. Then came Brother André and Father Wendolin. Brother Dutton was last. After Dutton prayed and made his sign of the cross, he laid his hand on my shoulder and said, "May the peace of the Lord be with you."

I thought tears would come easily for me but they didn't.

After all who would come had paid their respects, Sam asked those lingering few to step outside while the coffin was closed.

When the cottage was empty, Sam and I, Makana, Rico, A`ai, and Kamalani stood around Hiapo with our hands locked. Sam spoke about how Hiapo brought life into the house, how he lived life with a light of joy and how he filled all those near him with the love.

Rico offered a prayer in Portuguese, then he twined the rosary his family gave him around Hiapo's hand. A`ai's farewell was silent. He simply pinned his Rifles Medal on Hiapo's lapel. Kamalani draped Hiapo with the ilima lei. Then we all stepped back and Sam and I closed the casket.

We loaded the casket on the buggy, and Sam and I led the procession of mourners to church. The healthy walked and the lame limped up the hill toward the call of the bells where altar boys with crippled hands slipped their forearms through the loops of the bell rope and tolled the bells by pulling down with their elbows.

Sam and I sat in the first pew. I sat closest to the aisle. To my right was Hiapo's coffin. The altar boys marched out and draped the coffin with a silken black sheet. Some mourners came forward and touched the drape or lifted it to their mouths to kiss it before they took their places in the pews.

To my left, in an isolated wing of the church, were the mourners who were in advanced stages of the disease. Segregated by choice, they entered through the side door. Each took a banana leaf from the basket at the door entry. They rolled their leaves into tight tubes and poked them into square holes on the floor next to their kneelers. When drool flowed from their lips without any control, they put their mouths to the leaves and the saliva dripped down the leaves into the holes on the ground.

The priests and brothers waited at the front door until the organist struck the first chord. The congregation, those who could, stood when the clergy walked in two by two. The altar boys began the procession. They swung incense burners that sent pungent smoke curling toward the ceiling—it wrapped around the white-painted walls and enveloped the congregation in an all-consuming cloud.

Out of the smoke came the priests who walked down the aisle with their hands clasped over black satin vestments that were trimmed in gold. They sang Latin hymns as they walked, keeping their eyes focused blankly ahead, not looking at any of us as they passed.

Father Wendolin walked up the steps of the altar, bowed toward the crucifix, then turned to welcome the congregation. The lace of his sleeves was frayed and his vestments had green grass stains at the knees.

Brother André placed a gold chalice on the altar. The linen that covered the altar was yellowed and stained, and the altar statues had faces of peeling paint. The church was a jumble of color and disrepair.

The organist played, the patients sang, and the priest prayed with his back toward the congregation. I remember closing my eyes and letting the comfort of their song soothe me. I remember the organist's directions. All rise. Please sit. Kneel. Begin the exit.

I stood taking my place as a pall bearer. We lifted the coffin into the buggy. It was so light. I remember feeling the thud of Hiapo's body when one side of the casket dropped low as we loaded it into the buggy.

As I walked behind the carriage I swatted flies from my face. The mud on the road sucked at my shoes. I took in a strong whiff of the horse manure on the road and I smiled knowing that Hiapo was probably complaining.

We stood at his graveside. Sam stood behind me, resting his hands on my shoulders. Makana stood next to me, clasping my hand. I watched as Father Wendolin kneeled to scoop dirt into a rolled ti leaf. He rose slowly and gently sifted the dirt to form a cross on the top of Hiapo's coffin.

We prayed over the body one last time, then we lowered him into the ground.

* * *

The brothers spared no time in stripping Hiapo's bed and emptying his dresser. His trunk was shipped to his family, and the photo of him with his family was placed on my dresser.

There were times when I was walking to the stable, or passing the mango tree with our tree house, that I could almost feel his weight on my back and his fingers clutching at my neck. Sometimes when I cut through the coconut grove I listened for his voice.

I remember when I was a child lying in bed as still as I could so I could listen for my parents' voices as they talked over the events of the day or read to each other from the Bible. I would hold my breath and cock my head, trying to catch their every word. It was the same way I was listening for Hiapo.

I knew I would always feel his presence—when I walked the beach, when I watched the soaring `iwa. I knew he was there—but I knew I would never be able to touch him again. It was at night that I missed Hiapo most—when I would wait for his giggle or whispers in the dark.

I spoke to no one and developed a quick hatred for the new boy in Hiapo's bed. He was a *haole* boy, a missionary's son who was born in Shanghai.

I lost hope. I let the cold rains drench me when I walked. I let days go by not leaving my bed. The sun was setting earlier, stealing more and more of each day. I didn't leave the compound and hadn't been back to the clinic for a week. I refused visits from Sam and `Ōpūnui, and I took to my bed even more.

My thoughts turned to Paka and I became obsessed with wondering about the bodies the sheriff had found. I fantasized about climbing the trail and looking at the bodies myself. I refused to believe that Paka was dead, but with the rain getting colder and the wind whirling from the valley, I almost hoped he was.

One early morning I walked out toward Mōkapu Island, toward Pelekunu Valley. Some patients were fishing in their *malo*. Poised on rocks near the ocean, they cast perfect circles of their nets. The sea birds were flying and a sliver of the moon was a faint white shadow on the morning sky.

As the sun got higher, the scrub brush took on a silver shine and a cool rain fell. The cliffs took on green and black shadows, and I could almost see the upside-down waterfall at Wailele.

From the promontory I could hear the Pelekunu's moan. The stones rumbled over the sand and a blue cloud lay in wait in the valley. I thought I heard a howling spirit in the mist. I pictured it poised to pounce on my soul.

I wanted to challenge the ghost, to test myself and prove myself a man. I wanted to face death squarely and I wanted it to consume me. Then I could die in glory.

I pictured myself swimming out to the mouth of the valley, placing myself at the mercy of the spirits and begging them to thrash my body against the rocks. I conjured the scene in my mind—the surf tossing me, crashing over me—I saw the wave flood over me—its light bubbles of white sizzling foam.

Then I knelt on the shore, cradling my knees, for what was a long time.

I went back to the dorm and stayed in bed, missing the evening meal. The next day I didn't get up. I spoke to no one and slept for most of the day. I refused to leave my bed and ate only when ordered to do so.

It was later that I found out it was Brother Dutton who got word about me to Sister Augustine. I heard her voice on the verandah as she greeted the boys. Her voice was almost singing.

I turned my head away from the door and pretended I was asleep.

"Loa." Her voice was definite and demanding. Her shoes banged as she barreled her way to my bed. "Get up, Loa."

I was forced to open my eyes.

"It's good to see you, Loa," she said.

I didn't speak.

"Loa, if you don't get up, you'll wither away and die." Her voice was stern, but her face showed fear and concern.

"You're just inviting death," she said.

"The *lēpela* will take care of my death."

"Get up, I said." Her breath was warm and smelled of mint.

"Leave me alone."

"Loa, I will not allow you to do this to yourself," she said.

"You can't stop me," I said.

"I'm here to try," she said.

"Who asked you to come?"

"I'm not here because anybody asked me."

I laid on my back staring at the ceiling. "Then why did you

come?"

"Because I'm scared," she said.

"Go away." I turned away and covered myself with my sheet. "Let me die in peace."

"Loa, I'm begging you, don't do this."

"Don't waste your begging, Sister."

She pulled the sheet off me. "I said get up!"

I didn't move.

She rattled the bed. "Why are you so intent on wasting your life? You're killing yourself."

I laid still, ignoring her.

"Answer me!" She grabbed my shoulders. "Or is it just plain self-pity?"

I stared at her blankly.

"There are boys here who would give anything to have your strength. You have a lot of life ahead of you."

"How do you know how much life I have left?" I asked.

"For me, Loa, please. Will you get up for me?"

I could hear tears in her voice. "Why do I have to get up so you can feel better about yourself?" I yelled. "I'm the one who is dying."

"I know," she cried.

"No, you don't know! Only I know!" I screamed. "I'm the one dying, not you."

The tears finally came. I felt my body give in and my tears poured out. The tears, the mourning, the fear, the anger, all of it—I took hold of it and faced the terror . . . I was going to die.

"I don't want to die," I said. I drew in shallow gasps of air and clenched my pillow. I felt the Sister's arms around me. She cradled me like a child.

"I don't want to die," I said in a whisper, "and no one can do a thing about it." I let the tears flow slowly.

"Loa, I don't know why God allows the things he does." She rubbed my back as she spoke. "Sometimes it's hard not to question."

"Sometimes death is so routine for me that when I am singing the Song of the Dead over a coffin, I'm thinking about how many bandages I need to order or how much liniment we have." She pulled a handkerchief from her habit sleeve and wiped tears from her face. "But sometimes a boy like Hiapo . . . or you . . . comes along and I end up questioning if there even is a God, after all."

"It's not fair," I said, sitting up.

"Fair or not, sometimes we have to accept things. God has a plan for us, even if we can't see it," she said.

"What was the plan for Hiapo?" I asked. "To die at eight years old?"

"I don't know, William, that's part of faith."

"No god cares," I said.

She held my hand.

"The *lēpela* doesn't care." I looked up at Sister. "It didn't care that I was going to be a doctor, or that Rico has a family, or that everyone loved Hiapo. It doesn't care if you're the worst sinner or a little boy," I said.

"It's why I do God's work here, William. It's his plan for me," she said. "And I just accept it."

"So I should accept my *lēpela?*" There was anger in my voice.

"I'm saying you should try to see God's plan," she said.

* * *

I visited the clinic the next day. `Ōpūnui was tending to patients in the ward, and when I asked about Kamalani I was told she was in the convent helping the sisters for the annexation commissioners' visit. It wasn't until dinner later that night that I would see her.

I rode up to Makana's cottage. They were outside waiting to welcome me back with aloha.

Kamalani was already there. She wasn't so quick with her warmth. She used her best parlor manners when she spoke to me, and when I complimented her on her biscuits she accused me of being arrogant. The dinner was more quiet than usual. Mr. A`ai had a touch of lung fever and Rico was in bed, hung over.

It was a formal meal. Sam and Makana asked me few questions and Kamalani continued to be cold.

For days afterward at the clinic Kamalani addressed me as "Mr.

Ka`ai" and nodded her head when I asked how she was.

Then Sister Augustine ordered me to help Kamalani haul the bandage cart to the laundry. The cart rumbled and the wheels banged against stones in the road. The ocean was calm that day— the waves rolled in and doves cooed to each other, almost mocking the two of us as we worked, not speaking.

I watched Kamalani as she tucked her apron up under her belt and reached into her pockets for gloves.

"Kamalani, I'm sorry," I said.

"You have no reason to apologize to me," she quipped.

"I don't know what happened to me, but it's finished," I said.

"What do you mean, Loa?"

"It's finished, that's all I can say."

I gently touched her arm. She pulled way. "I don't know why you're angry," I said.

"Don't you?"

"No."

She heaved a sigh of disgust.

"Will you please talk to me?" I said.

"Why didn't you talk to me?" she snapped back.

"What do you mean?"

"Why couldn't you talk to me about Hiapo?" There was hurt and anger in her voice. "Why couldn't you tell me what you were feeling? Do you think you're the only one who loved him?"

I wanted to hold her, but I was afraid she would be more angry if I tried. "Kamalani." I reached out my hand.

"Why do you think you're so special, Loa?" She knelt down next to the basket of bandages and began sorting them, tossing them into three different piles.

"Kamalani, listen to me." I knelt next to her.

"What?" The darkness of her eyes was softened by a film of tears.

"I can't explain what I don't understand myself. All I know is that whatever happened to me is over and I never wanted to hurt you."

"We all miss Hiapo," she said.

"It didn't have anything to do with Hiapo," I said. "Well, perhaps part of it did, but more of it was the *lēpela*," I said, as I helped her up. "I'm sorry, Kamalani," I said.

"Maybe I don't understand, Loa. But unless you talk me, I'll never be able to comfort you."

I held her.

"Loa, don't close yourself off to me," she whispered. "You're all I have here."

It was her comfort I was afraid of. If I took her comfort, I wouldn't be alone. If I took her comfort, then we would begin to share, to be part of each other.

I wanted to prove I could live alone, like Paka—survive with no one's help. Like Paka, I thought, alone, probably dead, and still with the *lēpela* hunting him down.

I didn't know what I wanted. I wanted her to love me and I wanted to tell her how afraid I was, but more than that, I wanted to protect her—to be a man, to be strong and protect her. But what I wanted to protect her from most, I had no control of. None of us had control.

Chapter 13

September 11, 1898

On September 11, 1898, the Annexation Commission visited Kalaupapa. Brother Dutton hoisted an American flag at the landing, the band played American marches, and the sisters lined up the young girls who were wearing new red, white, and blue *mu'umu'u*.

Kamalani was standing on the porch with the older girls, and each of them was holding a miniature American flag. Some of the girls waved their flags as the commissioners walked by, some curtsied and smiled.

'Ōpūnui nudged me and motioned toward Kamalani. She stood there with her arms crossed, her hips tilted, clenching the American flag in her fist.

"Tough, your woman," 'Ōpūnui said.

Her head was cocked and her hat was pulled down over her eyes.

"Loa." Sister Augustine pointed to a man in a black derby hat. One of the man's legs was shorter than the other and he walked with a cane. "He'll need some help climbing into the buggy," she said. "Could you please arrange it?"

`Ōpūnui whispered in my ear, "I think you should help him yourself. Offer him that crooked hand of yours and we'll see how fast he can move with that cane."

"I'll see to it, Sister," I said.

"I dare you," `Ōpūnui said.

Almost everyone in the settlement was gathered in front of the parade stand listening to speeches about "the victims of *lēpela*" and "the unfortunate few."

Two girls sitting on the dormitory steps started to fight over a doll, a few boys in the field were trying to lasso each other, and the band's drummer was sprawled out on the ground, asleep. A gust of wind lifted the superintendent's notes off the podium and spun them, sailing over the crowd.

Sister Augustine wrapped herself in her black shawl.

Clouds rolled out of the mountain ravines. They looked more like smoke from a brushfire than clouds.

One of the commissioners presented Brother Dutton with new boxing equipment for the boys. Mother Marianne was given a croquet set for the girls.

"Isn't that wonderful!" Sister Augustine said. "The children will get such pleasure from them." She tucked the ends of her shawl under her arms as she clapped.

The sky darkened and the wind picked up. Brother Dutton announced that due to the oncoming storm the ceremonies would be shortened. The American songs that the young girls practiced so long and the lasso demonstration by the Baldwin Home boys were cut from the program.

The commissioners, Dutton said, would be given a brief tour of Kalaupapa.

There was the smell of a great rain coming. The ocean turned a muddied green and the whitecaps could be seen out to the horizon.

The commissioners scurried to their buggies. The man with the black derby hat limped behind them.

"Go ahead," `Ōpūnui said. "I'll get you fresh poi and rum if you offer the *haole* your hand."

"Fresh poi, not dried."

"Fresh," he repeated.

"Delivered to me next week?" I asked.

"Tell me which day and you'll have it," he said.

I took `Ōpūnui's cotton gloves.

"I think that commissioner should know I'm a friend of the Queen." I winked. "Yes, the Queen thinks I am a gifted young man." I rolled the lapels of my jacket and pulled down my sleeves. "I've read poetry for her, you know."

"So I have heard." `Ōpūnui smiled.

I headed straight toward the commissioner, and looking him directly in the eye, I extended my gloved hand and said, "May I help you?"

He averted his eyes away from me. I took a step closer. He took a step back.

"I'd like to help you up," I said. I moved so close to him I knew he could feel the heat of my breath.

"No, thank you, I can manage," he said.

At first he looked away from me. He looked anywhere but at my face—at the band, at `Ōpūnui, at the field. Then after his first quick glance at my face, he couldn't look anywhere else. He fixed on me and I watched as he blatantly stared at my disease.

Look at me, I wanted to say. Look at me, not the *lēpela*. I'm no different than you.

"No, the others will help me," he said.

He's the diseased one, I thought. Him and his smiling friends.

He nodded and nervously smiled.

It was the man's smile, like a painted mask that protected him from me—it was his smile that angered me the most. It held in his fear and kept his terror from showing. He smiled at me like it was an act of honor on his part, or perhaps a grand gesture of compassion. He was smiling at one of the "unfortunates," one of the "unclean," as he cowered away from me, avoiding any possibility of my touch.

One of his colleagues helped him board the buggy.

"Have a good tour," I said, waving as I watched their buggy move on. The carriage zigzagged across the road, avoiding the deep ruts and stones set in the road by Royalists.

The superintendent waved to residents in their front yards and stopped for the commissioners to talk to those very few residents he knew supported the annexation.

I wondered if the annexation commissioners had noticed the quilts on the other cottage verandahs—the quilts clapping in the breeze with their brightly colored designs of the Hawaiian Kingdom, the King's seal and Queen Lili`uokalani's favorite crown flower. The buggy crested the hill, and at the Church of the Healing Water it turned back toward Kalaupapa.

The sky had a green cast to it. The wind became still and clouds shrouded the mountains. There was very little sound. No dogs barked. No birds cooed. And the leaves of the trees looked yellow.

The buggy made it back to the dock, and the commissioners ran straight to the ship holding their jackets closed and their hats on their heads. They scurried, like rats.

One of them, who had come back to talk to Dutton, dashed around me as he ran. He was wearing a gray suit and had on steel-rimmed spectacles. As he ran he left behind a stench of Bay Rum and wet wool.

The commissioners boarded their vessel and the visit was over. Sam, Makana, Kamalani, and I headed back to the cottage. The rain began to fall, gently at first, and then, within minutes, great torrents of cold rain pounded us.

Sam took off his jacket and covered Makana's head and shoulders. Kamalani and I ran ahead. The wind whipped at my face.

Kamalani and I ran faster, heads down, hand in hand, up the hill. We jumped over branches tumbling across the road and dashed through a whirl of bougainvillea. The wind lifted the petals, tainted white and blood-red, as they showered us with a fury of color.

Kamalani stamped her feet on the porch and shook the rain off her bonnet. "I'm soaked through."

"Just in time," Rico called from inside the house. "Two minutes later and A`ai would have been dead."

"Murdered by a madman," A`ai yelled out.

"Hurry!" Kamalani leaned over the railing and waved to Sam and Makana. She pointed to the churning waterfalls. "Hurry!"

Rico brought us towels, and we took off our shoes and dried our faces and hands. By the time Sam and Makana made it back, there were rivulets flowing though Makana's flower garden.

In the cottage A`ai was sitting in the living room rocker, facing out the back window. "They're coming," he said.

"You're crazy, Hawaiian," Rico said.

Kamalani held A`ai's hand. "Who's coming A`ai?"

"Look." He pointed toward the valley. "In the fog . . . they're coming."

Rico made the sign of the cross. "He's been like this all morning—muttering about dead souls in blue clouds. I swear I'm going to kill him myself." Rico opened the back door, but a blast of wind slammed it shut against him.

"Where are you going?" Makana asked him.

"To tie things down," he said.

"Wait, and I'll help you." Sam took off his jacket and headed toward the kitchen, to the bedroom behind it, but Rico went out and I started down the stairs after him.

We tied down the water casks to the porch rail and put the chairs in the shed. A dark gray cloud was moving in from the bay.

"Get in here, you two," A`ai yelled from the window. "Get in the house before they get you."

"Crazy fool," Rico mumbled. "He's sure death is coming today."

"Maybe the laudanum made him delirious," I said.

"He's just crazy," Rico said.

Sam had changed into his work clothes. Together we boarded up the windows while Rico gathered up his gardening tools. We worked quickly. The rain was heavy and loud and the yard quickly turned into mud. The herbs in Rico's garden were uprooted and the croton bushes were bent over.

The rain pounded on the metal roof.

Rico yelled, "Help me cut these." He bent over the croton with his machete and sliced them to the ground. Hacking them down was the only way to save them, or they would be uprooted, too, and die.

Sam was tying up the poles from the wedding tent and sliding them under the house.

"What about the swing?" I shouted to Sam.

"It's all right, it's heavy."

By the time we got back in the house the clouds had moved in and it was as dark as dusk.

"You'll all catch a death of cold," Makana said, as she rubbed Sam's face and arms with a towel.

Rico was heading back out the door again. "My netting needles," he said.

"Stay inside. I'll get them," I said.

"You stay inside." He swung his forearm in front of me, but I brushed it away.

I ran down the steps, almost slipping. Over the rains I could hear A`ai yell, "Now look what you've done, Cabral. You've killed the boy."

I ran out to the eucalyptus tree and got Rico's needles. The branches bounced and creaked. When I made it back into the house, Rico cradled his needles.

Kamalani and Makana were all settled in, wrapped in blankets. The wind hissed through the cracks in the walls, blowing the curtains to the ceiling.

"It's going to be a bad one," Rico said, looking through the X-crossed lumber covering the windows.

"It's death, I tell you," A`ai said.

The windows rattled and jars of jams and jellies clinked on the shelves.

"Sam." Rico called him to the window. "Look."

I went too. There were people staggering on the road, bent over against the wind, some slipping in the mud.

Sam went out the back door and got his shoes.

"Where are you going?" Makana said.

"They need help, Makana," Sam said, as he was lacing up his shoes.

"Don't," she said. "Please, Sam. Just this once, let someone else go."

I got my boots and Rico's.

"I'll be all right, Makana," Sam said.

Makana turned to me. "Loa, you are not going out there."

"He's a man, Makana. He speaks for himself," Sam said.

"Don't worry, Makana." Rico put his hand on her shoulder. "I'll watch out for him. I promise, no harm will come to the boy."

"I'll get the lanterns," I said.

A`ai moaned about the devil winds that were rising out of the bay. "Through the blue veil of dusk it comes. Out of the stillness it blows. The souls of the dead shrouded in the fog."

Kamalani sat next to him, soothing him.

When we opened the front door, a wind blew through the house, smashing Makana's vase to the floor, spilling water and flowers and splintered glass.

Makana looked at Sam. "Be careful," she said

I stepped onto the verandah. The wind hit me and I lost my balance.

Father Wendolin was hollering from the road. He cupped his hands and shouted above the rain. He waved his arms and pointed up the hill.

"The stables," he yelled. "The stables."

"Fire," a man shouted from the road.

The three of us made it out toward the priest. The mud was slippery and the wind pelted my face.

"The stable is on fire," Father Wendolin yelled.

Part of the roof from the Na`ope's cottage lifted and smashed into the trees.

I turned back to the cottage to see a silhouette of Makana at the door. A gust came up, I lost my balance and in trying to keep myself from falling, I dropped the lantern. It rolled down the road, and I chased after it leaning over, with my arms dangling, trying to swipe it up.

I got it at the crest of the hill. From the Church of the Healing Water, I couldn't see Saint Philomena's, there were just sheets of rain, pelting down in torrents. Once on the other side of the hill, I could see the coconut trees and after I was through the grove, I saw the smoke from the stable.

I headed straight for the lines of men in the middle of the quad. I took my place in the line, passing buckets of water and buckets of sand, man to man. My arms ached and blood from my hands mixed with the rain, forming thin red puddles in my palms.

Sam was digging sand, filling the buckets.

Lum Kup called Rico to the stable.

The fire raged, and through the wall of rain I saw shadows of men leading horses out of the stable. Orange flames burned through the smoke.

Some brothers stood in the line with me, others were leading some boys out of the dormitories closest to the stable.

Tree branches snapped off and flew through the air like javelins. The wind shifted and the smoke blew in my direction.

"Loa."

I thought I heard my name above the rain.

"Loa."

"Loa, over here." It was Brother Luis.

"The dormitory."

The roof of a dormitory was rising off its wall. The shingles spun like leaves, and the roof itself flapped like the wings of a frantic bird.

"Check it," he shouted. "Make sure no boys are inside."

It was a relief to be out of the rain. I wiped my face dry and slid my hands down my sleeves, showering the floor with water. I wrung out my pants legs and looked around for a dry jacket I could wear.

Then I felt it—the floor pitched and there was a loud bang, like a great gun, then cracking, followed by sounds of splintering, ricocheting from every wall. The roof beam split and the walls were collapsing and the floor was lifting in rhythmic waves. I ran, patting down every bed and checking underneath them.

The roof beam was sagging as I rushed for the door. The floor started to lift. There was another bang and the beam collapsed, the roof began to cave in. I headed out the door. The walls were giving way. Wood ripped and splintered, glass shattered. I ran down the stairs and fell in the mud. I tried to stand to run away.

There was a crashing thud, but it sounded more like an explosion, then a cloud of soot and the dormitory collapsed.

I ran under the banyan tree. Blood ran over my eyes, my hands were slit, and I had a gash on my leg.

Rain surged through the compound.

I huddled under the tree, curled low against the wind, watching planks of chicken coops and bodies of dead chickens sweep by. I shut my eyes and tucked my head in my shoulder.

The bells of Saint Philomena's were clanging wildly. I heard the sound of my name over the bells.

"Loa!" It was Sam. "Loa! Come!"

He was headed toward the kitchen with a sack on his back.

I followed behind him. Brother Luis leaned against the door helping Sam in. Sam and Brother Luis lowered the bloody sack slowly to the floor. But it wasn't a sack, it was a body wrapped in a blanket. It was Rico. His face was misshapen and his skull was caved in.

Sam knelt beside his friend and held Rico's head in his lap.

"He was helping to get the horses out of the barn when a beam fell on him," Brother Luis said.

There was blood dripping from his nose and ears. Rico moved his lips. *"Deus me perdoe."* God forgive me, Rico said.

Rico tried to raise his head, and Sam leaned close to him. Rico's face was strained as he tried to speak. He closed his eyes as if he were trying to suffer through a pain beyond what he could endure.

Rico gripped Sam's shirt. "You promised me," he said.

"I promise," Sam said.

"Promise me." Rico's hands were blue and swollen. "Deep."

"I'll bury you deep—high on the crater hill," Sam said. "So high you will be able to see Maui and you can watch your kids grow."

Rico's body jerked and he let his head fall back and rest in Sam's hands.

"And Makana will plant basil around your plot," Sam said.

There was a rattle of Rico's last breath and his eyes were lifeless.

"I'll write to your wife. I won't tell her what an old goat you were."

Sam rocked Rico's limp body. "You gave me such a hard time, old man, when A`ai dies I should bury him right next to you." Sam laughed through his tears. "That's what I should do— I'll put his coffin on top of yours, so the two of you can fight forever."

I knelt next to Sam and put my arm around him.

"Who's left for me to talk to, my friend?" Sam held onto Rico's hand.

Brother Luis tucked a pillow under Rico's head. "He has the angels to fight with now, Sam," Brother Luis said.

In the middle of the storm, with the sounds of men yelling orders to each other, with the smoke of the fire drifting through the cracks, with the rain pounding on the roof, we paused, and Brother Luis prayed over Rico's body.

He put his hand on Rico's forehead, he closed Rico's eyes and crossed Rico's hands over his body. We knelt in silence, responded to the Brother's prayers, and waited before we wrapped Rico's body.

Sam took off Rico's shoes and socks. The skin on his feet peeled like wet paper. I watched as Sam dabbed Rico's feet with a towel. He moved like he was anointing the feet of a king. He touched him gently, the whole time talking in a soothing voice.

"I will miss you, my friend," Sam said. *"Aloha nō."*

* * *

The next morning the settlement was littered. There were houses that leaned into trees, and parts of chicken coops and quilting looms were strewn in piles. Vegetable crops floated in puddles, gravestones were smashed, buggies were in pieces, and dogs scavenged through debris.

Makana's cottage was still standing. The roof sagged a bit, but it was sound. Her flower garden was gone, her flowerpots were in pieces, and the new back yard swing was destroyed.

It was the Church of the Healing Water that suffered most. Almost all of the building had slid into the ocean. Its bell had rolled into the rocks, and by noon that day a chain of men had hoisted it back to shore. The church bell that had rung for weddings and funerals and the birthday of the Queen was gouged by rocks and pounded by the sea.

I sat on the water cask on Makana's front porch. Perhaps A`ai was right. Perhaps a band of spirits did come through.

"Loa, did you hear that?" Kamalani opened the screen door. "There it is again," she said.

I shook my head no. "I didn't hear anything."

"It sounds like a beam is cracking," she said. "I think it's coming from the roof."

"It's nothing, Makana," I said.

"It sounds like wood tearing from nails," she insisted.

"Have you asked Sam about it?" I asked.

"He says it's the back wall," she answered. "But I'm sure it's the roof."

"I'll look at the roof later," I said.

From where I sat I counted fourteen buggies buried in the mud. The cottage across the street stood at a lean.

Kamalani came outside. "Sam asked me to get you, Loa. He needs help with Rico's body."

"I'll be right in."

I kept thinking about the church bell. I imagined I could hear it rolling along the ground, clanging against the stones. I wondered what kind of wedding ceremony Rico had had. Church bells probably rang, I thought, and he probably had a grand party.

That day was the clearest I ever saw at the settlement. The mountains were green, there wasn't a cloud in the sky. It was so clear that from the porch I could see the waterfall near our getaway cave.

Before going in the house, I scooped some water to drink from the cask. It tasted like acid brown wood.

A`ai had lined up all our shoes. He stuffed them with newspaper and put them on the floor in the sun.

The cottage was quiet. No one spoke much. Kamalani washed the mud out of our clothes. Makana pressed Rico's white shirt with an iron heated by charcoal, and the smell of his shirt being steamed filled the cottage. It smelled like sweet lavender. Sam and I washed Rico's body. Rico still smelled like cigars. How strange, I thought, that a dead man would smell of cigars.

When I looked in his dresser to get a pair of clean socks, I found a scribbled note, *"Aqui me vejo solitario lutando con men fadario."* Here I am alone struggling with my fate.

I took the photo of Rico's family off the wall and brought it out to be placed in his coffin. Sam and I lifted Rico's body into the casket and rested his head on an embroidered pillow. We sat vigil with him, one of us, all through the night. And in the morning we took our place in a long line of buggies and carts that were filled with the bodies of the dead from the storm.

Coffins jammed the church aisles. Some bodies were laid out without coffins on bare planks of raw wood.

Once again the priests processed in wearing their black robes, the altar boys covered us with incense smoke, the church bells clanged, and the congregation recited the prayers for the dead.

I looked out the window beyond Damien's grave, beyond the cemetery, toward Kalawao Bay. Hundreds of white cross markers were strewn across the field. Chiseled stone memorials were cracked and split. Beyond the cemetery and the trees I could see Kalawao Bay and the Pelekunu Valley.

Perhaps A`ai was right, from out of the valley the spirits did come. Death had come and it did devour us.

There was a double rainbow arching between Mōkapu and Pelekunu, and I remembered the day Hiapo and I sat eating peanuts in the tree house.

"May the love of God give us comfort on this day," Father Wendolin began to pray.

"Can you see the rainbow, Hiapo?" I whispered. It was a brilliant rainbow that shone with clear colors.

Hiapo, do you remember the day we saw the double rainbow? This one is even brighter.

"May we be each other's comfort," Father Wendolin continued. "May we be each other's joy."

Did I give you comfort, Hiapo? For sure, you were my joy.

"On this day that God has given us may we rejoice in Him," the priest said.

I miss you, Hiapo. There are times I want to hear your voice so badly, even though I know you would probably be complaining about the cart, or the food, or your kite not flying high enough. I miss you, Hiapo.

I looked over at Sam and Makana. They stood close to each other, holding each other's hands. They are each other's comfort, I thought. And they are each other's joy.

I turned to Kamalani and I watched as the shadow of the plumeria fluttered across her face. I breathed in the sweet smell of its blossoms and I closed my eyes.

Is there really a heaven, Hiapo? Or is this our heaven here?

I opened my eyes and reached for Kamalani's hand.

Two pews ahead of us were A`ai and `Ōpūnui. Across the aisle were Sister Augustine, the priests, and the brothers. The boys from the dormitory were in front of them, and men from the stable stood at the side door.

I looked over to `Ōpūnui—`Ōpūnui, who had taught me how to heal.

I looked at Sister Augustine who showed me courage, to Brother Luis who taught me compassion, to Kamalani who taught me love.

This is it, Hiapo, isn't it? We truly are each other's comfort, and we are each other's joy. Today is a beautiful day, Hiapo.

And the day I die will be as beautiful as it is today. But today I am alive and today I am loved.

Today at Kalaupapa

I married Kamalani in May of 1900. Mr. A`ai didn't live to see us marry. He died of lung fever two months before the wedding.

Before A`ai died he sent to Honolulu for a coral gravestone. It was in the shape of a cross. At its base was an inscription that read:

Enrico Sandro Cabral
Beloved Father, Husband and Friend
Born 1865 Madeira
Died 1898 Kalawao

After our wedding Kamalani and I lived with Sam and Makana in their cottage. We continued our work at the hospital, and at nineteen I became the chief medical assistant and Kamalani was the head nurse's aide.

On October 21, 1903, Sam died of the *lêpela* and Makana moved to Bishop Home to help the sisters care for the girls. Kamalani and I lived in the cottage alone for many years.

In 1930, at age eighty-eight, Brother Dutton left the settlement for an eye operation in Honolulu. While he was there in the hospital he heard a radio for the first time.

Dutton died in Honolulu. His body was brought back to Kalawao and he was buried next to Damien in the cemetery of Saint Philomena's.

Today Kalaupapa is still home to Hansen's disease patients who stay there voluntarily. The isolated peninsula settlement is their home.

The Sisters of Saint Francis still staff the hospital at Kalaupapa. Sister Evelyn Nicholas has been caring for patients for thirty-seven years. Every Tuesday and Thursday you can find her fishing at the tidal basin, just west of Mad Nehoa's cottage.

From a distance she looks like a white butterfly perched on the black rock. When she leans back to cast her line, her sleeves billow and her veil snaps in the wind. She squints to follow her line in the sun. She tucks her white habit between her legs and leans forward resting her elbows on her knees, bracing her muddied sneakers against the rocks.

As she sits facing Kalawao Bay, Sister Evelyn Nicholas is a familiar sight—surrounded by her blue cooler, a yellow plastic bucket, and her rusted old tackle box. The sea is calm, the sky is blue, the frigate birds soar, and Sister Evelyn Nicholas hums a Hawaiian song.

Today, there can be no more beautiful a day at Kalaupapa.

Glossary

Words are Hawaiian unless otherwise noted.

auē An exclamation that can be translated "Oh dear!" or "Too bad!" It also can be the sound of wailing, moaning, or grieving. In this book it is used both as a sound of wailing and of great despair.

'ehu A clay-color red tinge in the hair of Polynesians. Sometimes the word is used to describe the reddish skin color of some Polynesians.

hala A pandanus tree, native from Asia east to Hawai'i. The aerial roots of this tree look like poles supporting the trunk of the tree. It is said that the first night Father Damien spent in Kalaupapa he slept under the pandanus tree next to Saint Philomena's church. The leaves *(lauhala)* are woven and used in making mats, baskets, and hats.

hālau A long house used for canoes or hula instruction; also refers to a hula school or a hula troupe. At Kalawao the girls of the Baldwin Home had their own hula *hālau* and performed for visiting dignitaries and local celebrations.

haole White person, American, Englishman, Caucasian. The word is sometimes used to define any foreigner. The word *haole* as it refers to white people sometimes is written and pronounced *"ha ole,"* meaning without breath. Breath is a spiritual life force for Hawaiians.

hapa A portion or part. The word is commonly used to describe someone of mixed blood. *Hapa haole,* for example, would be someone who is half-white.

haupia A sweet pudding made with coconut cream. In the late 1800s *haupia* was thickened with arrowroot. It is the traditional dessert for a lu`au.

heiau A pre-Christian place of worship. Usually a *heiau* is a terraced area with stones surrounding it. *Heiau* usually have specific purposes; for example, a *heiau ho`ōla* is a *heiau* for treating the sick.

he`e A squid or octopus.

holokū A Hawaiian woman's dress that was modeled after the missionary women's dresses. It had a yoke front and a train. *Holokū,* as opposed to *mu`umu`u,* were worn for more formal occasions.

hui A club, association, or society. *Hui* may be formed for business purposes, like a syndicate, or a *hui* may be a group who form a hiking club or a volunteer organization.

huli To turn over or curl over. A boat turning over in the water would be said to *huli,* as is meat being turned over when being cooked over a grill.

`iwa Frigate bird.

kahuna Priest, minister, sorcerer, expert in any profession. Medical *kahuna* practiced during the time of this book. A resurgence in interest in traditional Hawaiian medical training has occurred today.

kanikau Lamentation, chant of mourning, grieving wail. The sound of Loa's mother crying *"auē,"* was a *kanikau.* She was grieving the loss of her son.

kiawe The algaroba tree. It was first planted in Hawai`i in 1828 and has become one of the most common and useful trees. One of the more common uses is as cooking wood. The algaroba tree is also know as a mesquite tree.

kōnane   A traditional Hawaiian game, similar to checkers.

kukui   Candlenut tree, a large tree bearing nuts containing white, oily kernels. The nut was used as a candle; at night fishermen would light the shore using *kukui*. The nut is slightly larger than a walnut. *Kukui* nuts are used for lei for men. The deep black nuts are polished to a high gloss, then strung.

kūlolo   A sweet pudding made of baked or steamed grated taro *(kalo)* and coconut cream.

laua`e   A fragrant fern that, when crushed, smells like *maile*.

lauhala   Leaf of the pandanus tree. *Lau* means leaf. See *hala*.

lēpela   Leprosy, a disease now known as Hansen's disease.

**liliko`i**   Passion fruit, a purple water lemon. The vine has dull-purple edible fruit, about two inches long. It grows wild in many forests of Hawai`i.

limu   A general name for all plants living under water as well as algae growing in the air, such as on rocks. Seaweed.

lomi   To rub, press, squeeze, massage; to work in and out.

machete   A Portuguese word. A small four-stringed guitar brought to Hawai`i by Portuguese immigrants. The *machete* was known as a *braguinha* or *machete* in Madeira, and as a *cavaquinho* in the Azores and continental Portugal. In Hawai`i it became `ukulele ("jumping flea") for the fast fretting fingers on the short neck.

maile A native twining shrub with shiny, fragrant leaves, used for decoration and leis. A *maile* lei is given for special occasions.

malo Loincloth worn by men.

mochi A Japanese word. Sweet, short-grained rice with a high starch content. The rice cakes made from this rice are commonly referred to as *mochi*. The rice is pounded with mallets until it becomes sticky, then it is formed into balls or squares. *Mochi* is also a chewy dessert dusted with *mochi* flour.

mu`umu`u A woman's dress, long and loose fitting.

noni The Indian mulberry, a small tree or shrub with large, shiny leaves. *Noni* was used for dyes and medicinal purposes.

ōkole The buttocks.

**`ōkolehao**  Liquor distilled from ti root. `Ōkolehao* was distilled by patients at the settlement. Later the same word was used for a gin made of rice or pineapple juice.

**`opihi**  Any of several species of limpets. `Opihi* are prized food because of the difficulty in obtaining them; the meat has been likened to abalone.

pali Cliff, precipice; steep hill; full of cliffs.

paniolo Cowboy. There is a long tradition of cowboys in Hawai`i.

panipani Slang term for sexual intercourse.

pāpio The young stage of growth of the *ulua*; a fish.

pōpolo The native pokeberry. The *pōpolo* is a black berry.

puka   Hole or opening.

tūtū   Granny, grandma, grandpa. Common pronunciation for the Hawaiian word *kūkū*.

Acknowledgement

The path to writing this book was not a straight line. There were unexpected twists and turns. Sometimes I got lost, or chose to take a detour; sometimes friends took me down guided paths. To all those who walked with me during this project, I am forever grateful.

To Dale Madden, for his faith in this project. To Dot Saurer, for her encouragement. To Virginia Wageman, for her patience, her care in editing and her mentoring. To Makia Malo, for sharing his soul and exposing his heart. To his wife, Ann, for her linguistic sensitivity. To Sharlene Silva, for her reading this manuscript for audiotaping. To Hi`ilani Shibata and Sarah Wageman, for their professional expertise. To Solomon Kiakona, for his explanation of statistical records kept on Hansen's disease patients. To the faculty of University of Hawai`i School of Library and Information Studies, for giving me the tools. To Dr. Jeanne Hoffman, for teaching me who the contenders really are. To Dr. John D. Haddock, for his explanation of animal behaviors. To Robert Mondoy and Reverend Nathan Mamo, for that first trip to Kalaupapa. To Dr. B. Alan Shoupe, for his review of surgical procedures, for his prayers, his care and his humor. To Evelyn Maldonado who shared her first-born, her *hiapo*, with the world for seven joy-filled years. To my son for his views on Loa. To my husband for his feedback and editing, for his delivering food and coffee to me in front of the computer and for not complaining despite months of missed meals and blank conversations.

To the Hawai`i State Public Library System, the University of Hawai`i Hamilton Library, Bishop Museum Library, Hawai`i State

Archives, Mission Houses Museum Library for use of their collections. Without access to their collections, this book could not have been written.

About The Author

Dorothea N. Buckingham, known as Dee, lives in Kailua, O`ahu, with her husband and son. Her first trip to Kalaupapa was in 1986. In 1989, while attending library school at the University of Hawai`i, she began researching the history of the settlement. Since that time she has made several trips to the settlement and has listened to many stories.

A share of royalties from this book will be given to Candlelighters Childhood Cancer Foundation, a support and education organization founded in 1970 by parents of children with cancer, and to HUGS (Help Understanding and Group Support), a Hawai`i organization that supports families of children with life-threatening diseases.